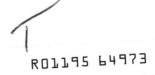

LAND OF THE FREE

THE SILVER FLEECE

THE
SILVER FLEECE

A Story of the Spanish in
New Mexico

By Florence Crannell Means
and Carl Means

Illustrations by Edwin L. Schmidt

THE JOHN C. WINSTON COMPANY

PHILADELPHIA • TORONTO

FIRST EDITION

MADE IN THE UNITED STATES OF AMERICA

Dedicated to the young Hulls,
MARY MARGARET
ANGUS CRANNELL
STEPHEN CARLETON
PETER HENRICH
JEREMY ROBERT

LAND OF THE FREE SERIES

Edited by Erick Berry

OTHER BOOKS BY FLORENCE CRANNELL MEANS

CONTENTS

CONTENTS

The Background of the Story

I
T WAS in the mid-fourteenth century, at a time when the empires of the conquered Aztecs and Incas were departing from living history that New Mexico was ushered in. The fires of this fresh Spanish conquest were kindled by tales told in old Spain, by Cabez a de Vaca and Fray Marcos, tales of fabulous treasures, of gold to be won for the conquerors and the Spanish crown, and of souls of pagan Indians to be won for the Roman Catholic Church. In 1540 a well-equipped expedition, led by Coronado, invaded North America. He was the first of the great explorers on the new continent, and his conquests gave to Spain and the Roman Catholic Church a vast new empire, and converts by the tens of thousands. But no gold.

Hard on the heels of the conquerors came colonization and the founding of the Franciscan missions. In 1598 Don Juan de Oñate, with four hundred soldiers and settlers, founded the first capital of New Mexico; this

1

was near the junction of the Chama and Santa Fe rivers on the site of a conquered Indian pueblo. He named it San Juan of the Gentlemen. A little later, after it was moved across the river, it was renamed San Gabriel. The third capital was established by Oñate's successor, Governor Peralta, and was called Santa Fe.

For countless thousands of years, since prehistoric times, the valley of the Rio Grande had been peopled by various tribes of Indians, agricultural, of different tongues and widely divergent stock. These the Spanish lumped together under the common name of Pueblos, for their vast communal adobe dwellings. On the fringes of the valley roamed nomadic tribes of Apaches, Comanches, Utes, Navajos, swooping down on pueblo, on Spanish town and hacienda, to kill and plunder, and with growing skill to drive off the cattle.

But the golden era of New Mexico's Franciscan missions ended in 1680. The Spanish influence had been weakened by the misrule of various later governors and by prolonged disagreement and conflict between civil and ecclesiastic authority. The Indians, stronger, and increasingly rebellious under the severity of the padres, who punished by floggings, imprisonments and death any participation in the ancient secret Indian rites, were roused by their medicine men into several revolts. For a while these failed for lack of unity. Then in 1680 a strong and able San Juan Indian named Popé united most of the Pueblos in a well-planned uprising. The plot was discovered, and the Spanish governor, Otermin, warned the settlers, some nine hundred of whom escaped to Santa Fe. But over four hundred of them did not reach the capital; they were killed, among them twenty-nine padres. Missions, chapels, Spanish dwellings were looted and burned.

After days of fruitless siege of the city of Santa Fe, the Indians cut off the town's primitive water supply on August 20. The Spanish assaulted their attackers, armed with guns against spear or bow and arrow, killed three hundred and took forty-seven captives, at the cost of only one Spanish officer and four soldiers. Next day Governor Otermin led his thousand refugees, ill-armed, ill-fed, ill-clad, out of the city and into the long-harrowing ten day's march to El Paso.

For twelve years thereafter the Indians held New Mexico, wiping out almost every trace of the hundred-year-old Spanish occupation. Only a few church and household treasures, buried by Indians faithful to their former white masters, were saved.

Then came the reconquest. This, in response to the challenge to restore the settlers to their homes and the Indians to Christianity, was led by Don Diego de Vargas. After many setbacks and long delays, he assembled a small force of Spanish soldiers and Indian allies and made his first excursion in August of 1692. They found many Indian pueblos deserted; the Indians, fearful of revenge, having fled their homes. Santa Fe was held by hostile Tanos, who had inclosed with fortlike houses the three sides of the square not already walled by the Governor's Palace. It took two weeks of conferences to reassure the Tanos and gain their surrender; De Vargas then visited seventeen pueblos, winning their apparent submission, while his priests baptized over two thousand Indians.

A year later came the second entrada; this was the formal reoccupation and resettlement of the Valley of the Rio Grande. The expeditionary force consisted of a hundred soldiers and seventy families, with their equipment and livestock. When they reached Santa Fe in December, they again found it hostile and snowbound. But they stormed and captured it with no Spanish deaths save from cold and hardship. De Vargas had also to make a second conquest of some of the pueblos. Not until 1695 could the "sixty-six and a half families" who had come up from Mexico City in 1694 refound and resettle Santa Cruz, twenty-five miles north of the capital.

Yet even then there was no permanent peace. In 1696 there was further Indian revolt, and while Santa Cruz weathered the storm, Fray Antonio Moreso and other priests were killed by the Indians they had loved and served. So for many years the balance of power wavered back and forth, the Indians always weakening, the Spanish growing ever stronger. And by the beginning of the eighteenth century the Pueblos had given up all hope of expelling the Spanish; they revolted no more. But for the next hundred and fifty years the nomadic Indians continued their devastating raids, until after New Mexico became part of the United States.

THE SILVER FLEECE

Chapter 1

A Big Hour

DOMINGO RIVERA lounged against the deep window sill and sniffed the April breeze.

He relished its cool freshness in the crowded Indian rooms; relished its scent of wild plum blossoms. Yet the other odors that rose from the Santa Fe plaza suited him even better. They were mingled smells of men and beasts and wood smoke and gunpowder, and all together they whetted the gentle spring air to an exciting edge of danger.

The Riveras were used to peril: Domingo and his twin sister, Lucia, who were in their sixteenth year, and their mother and uncle and aunt. Peril had traveled up from Mexico City with the Spanish when they returned from the old kingdom to the new after their years of exile. It had stayed with them during the months they had had to wait here in the capital, until the Indians had been quieted enough to make the resettling of outlying districts less deadly.

That sense of hazard still thrilled through the clamor in the plaza below. The squalling of the huge oxcart wheels mounted to a screech. The bray of mules, whinny of horses, fantastic pumping whoop of burros, yelp of dogs, redoubled. Above the din shrieked and shouted the voices of Spanish and Indians. A tremulous bleating, accompanied by the tintinnabulation of sheep bells, wove itself into the uproar.

"The flocks and herds will soon be setting out," Domingo commented.

His sister Lucia, perched on the adobe bench, flung down her mending and jumped to her feet as if jerked by his words. "Mother," she begged, "please let me go fetch Tuson de Plata!"

"Fetch him? Why would you fetch a lamb here?"

"I want to carry him in the carreta with us."

Doña Leonor shook her head, the serene oval of her face unruffled.

"But he is our hope for the future!" Lucia wailed. "It would bring us luck to let him ride into the New Town with us. Proudly! Practically under the banner of De Vargas!"

Domingo snorted. Doña Leonor's quiet mouth quirked with amusement, though she did not lift her gaze from her mending. "Your aunt would never in this world permit it," she said, her low-pitched voice soft, as if never quite let out. "Besides, your lamb is not weaned. Would you take his mother along in the carreta, also? The smell of their wool turns Tia Nina sick."

"The good wool!" Lucia reproached, her eyes filling with tears. "Oh, Mother, I do not want Plata to walk all the way. Twenty-five miles—it is too far. The rough road will wear out his poor hoofs. The journey might even stunt his growth once and for all."

Domingo grinned at his sister. She had only to quiver her chin and the tears flowed. Her mother regarded them skeptically; and Tia Nina was not affected by them, for she used the same device herself. Only Uncle Melchior still found Lucia's weeping potent. She was Uncle Melchior's one weakness.

Now she was stealing a glance in the mirror as if to see the effect. Domingo sprang to her side and twitched his own chin in vigorous mockery. Lucia's weeping was shattered by laughter as she looked at his face clowning over her head. Except for size, hair and eyes, the two were as near duplicates as two faces could be. Domingo's hair fell in a red-brown mane that almost touched his shoulders, like most of the men's, while Lucia's was long and heavy and demurely combed back. Domingo's eyes were deep brown, and Lucia's a startlingly light, bright blue between her black lashes.

"I never could make out how you could heave up those buckets of tears," Domingo hooted. "I could work at it for an hour and get never a drop."

"And you men do not need them," Lucia retorted resentfully. "The whole world belongs to you. Nobody ever questions your right to do as you please."

"But—Tuson de Plata! Fleece of Silver!" her brother mocked. "What a fancy name for a buck lamb!"

"Did you ever look at him?" Lucia demanded. "I mean really look at him? Not like the others. Every bit of him the loveliest soft white. Except one ear."

"In plain words, he is a plain white churro lamb with one plain gray ear," her brother said patronizingly.

"Not gray. Brown."

Domingo drooped amused lids at her.

"Do not tease your sister," Doña Leonor said, the phrase slipping out with the ease of frequent use. "Moreover, the name is a good one. And it is not so far-fetched to think that the small Silver Fleece might start our new fortune. Old Juan himself sets store by the criatura. Like enough he will let Silver ride on the burro's back with the sheep puppy, whenever he—"

"May I go and tell Old Juan to do that?" Lucia interrupted eagerly, reaching for her rebozo and flinging it round shoulders and head with practiced hand.

"With no servant to attend you?" Doña Leonor objected. "Rosa and Soledad are washing at the river, and Lupe has gone to the market for food. Domingo may go—"

"With pleasure," Domingo agreed.

He knelt quickly at his mother's feet and was up and away before the murmured blessing had left her lips. Swiftly he backed down the long ladder that was the stair of their temporary home.

This morning a good part of Santa Fe's thousand inhabitants had emptied out into the plaza, and Domingo murmured greetings right and left as he hurried across. Living here since last June, he had got acquainted with almost everyone, Spanish masters and peones, Tlascalan Indian servants from Old Mexico, and Tanos Indians, who had taken possession of the city after the Pueblos had risen and driven out the Spaniards fifteen years earlier. A miscellaneous assortment of other tribes gathered here also.

The Riveras had been best acquainted, however, with the sixty-six and a half families who had been their fellow travelers on the slow, hard trip up from Mexico City, and with whom they were now going on to resettle Santa Cruz, twenty-five miles to the north, and its environs, where were the Riveras' ancestral homes.

Here was Doña Ana, one of the neighbors whom they knew best and liked least. "How is it with you, Doña Ana?" Domingo asked politely. And here was Doña Ana's son, Salvador, big and glowering, with black hair falling into his eyes. He never glowered at Lucia; he stared at her admiringly. Domingo scowled at him now for all his past impertinences.

Everything had been arranged for the departure of the stock, and the formal proclamation was momentarily expected. Indeed, before Domingo could race across the plaza, the heightened tempo of the crowd told him that the great moment had come. He climbed on the lower rungs of a ladder so that he could see over the massed heads.

Rodríguez, the black drummer boy, stood proudly erect and awaited silence, looking very martial in his hat-shaped helmet, his boots and leggings, his trimly laced leather jacket. Few of the soldiers had metal armor, but the heavy leather was usually effective in stopping the Indian weapons.

The noise of the plaza dropped away, except for the cries and movement of animals. Rodríguez stood with chin high and eyes ahead, stock-still as a statue, until his audience was properly quiet. Then, after the trumpet call was repeated, he beat a stirring ruffle on his drum and whipped out a rolled paper. Dramatically unfurling it, he read it aloud in a ringing voice, while shivers of excitement chased each other up Domingo's spine.

Its high-sounding legal phrases proclaimed only what everyone knew. The Tanos Indians, who long ago seized Santa Cruz and the Canyon of the Neighbors, had been ordered the month before to leave their unlawful homes, and take new lands up the valley at Chimayó, or over at San Juan.

The most noble general and governor, Don Diego De Vargas Zapata Lujan Ponce de Leon, thereupon granted to the Spanish resettlers the village and its immediately surrounding lands and irrigation ditches. All details were set forth accurately, together with the officials who should rule and protect the place. Finally, the people were to set out the day after tomorrow, April 21, at ten o'clock in the morning.

The drummer's resonant voice fell quiet, and the previous babel rushed in to fill the emptiness it left, while drummer and band moved on to repeat the proclamation in the other plaza. The herds must get under way at once, since the journey would take much longer for them than for the people. A few armed soldiers would escort them and their drivers, for the stock was important. The Spanish colonists had brought to the country the first horses, the first pigs, the first sheep and even the first cats, but they had not quite succeeded in rooting them there at once. The wilder tribes of Indians were always alert to help themselves to these fabulous new creatures that added so much to the ease and interest of life.

As soon as Domingo could worm his way through the masses of people and animals, he went racing on again toward the Rivera corral, which lay beyond the ruins of the big adobe church southeast of the square. There he found Old Juan and Gaspar, the Navajo slave, pushing their preparations for departure.

Domingo's eyes searched the pitifully small flock for his sister's pet. Because she made such a fuss over the little creature, Domingo had always pretended a lordly indifference to Plata; but secretly he was interested. There was no danger of confusing Tuson de Plata with the other lambs that had been born overearly, for he was much larger than they, and he had a thicker, whiter fleece. He was the son of the son of the son of the patriarch of the old flock, the first Tuson de Plata, Fleece of Silver. In the Pueblo Revolt Old Juan had been forced to abandon his flock to the care of a Navajo woman servant, but he had stubbornly carried with him a buck lamb, son of that first Tuson, and a ewe lamb, one of Tuson's daughters. Through all the terror of flight, little Old Juan had lugged the lambs under his arms, thinking to breed up a new flock from these small beginnings. Domingo could not recall the event, occurring in his babyhood, but he had heard it all related a thousand times by Old Juan.

Now he caught sight of Silver, butting a famished little head against the nearest ewe, who pivoted coldly away from him. Domingo pushed through between the woolly bodies, picked up the lamb, and set it beside its own mother, recognizable by fleece as white as her son's. The lamb dropped on prayerful knees and applied himself eagerly to the udder.

"My mother says," Domingo reported to the shepherd, "that you may carry Plata on Raton's back if you like."

Bristling, Old Juan scowled up at Domingo. Old Juan had a twisted body and wrists as fleshless as gnarled cedar branches, and more courage than men twice his size. Wiry

gray hair stood out stubbornly from the brim of his battered hat; his ears flared like wings at each side of his
withered face; and his gray eyes snapped from under a
thatch of eyebrows.

Old Juan had many years ago come straight from Spain
to Grandfather Rivera. He had been a shepherd in the
old country, and wise even from his cradle in the ways
of the flock. Most of anything in the world he loved
Doña Leonor, the fatherless twins, and the sheep; but
with all his devotion he was independent and crotchety,
and argued every order that was given him.

"Undoubtedly it was the Señorita Lucia who coaxed
your lady mother," he grumbled. "The lamb should be
allowed to stretch his legs now and again. But if the
Señora commands—"

The furry burro, Raton, stood near by, drooping and
apparently headless. Old Juan had thrown his coat over
the creature's head, and as long as the garment remained
there, the burro would stand as if tied. Now, as Silver's
mother walked away from him, Old Juan reached for him
and swung him up into one of the leather saddlebags. Out
of the other saddlebag, peering across the medley of bag-
gage on the burro's back, Chepe, the sheep puppy, tilted his
baby head comically this way and that.

"There!" Juan fumed. "I hope the Señorita will be
satisfied. Is there anything more the Señorita would like
to say?"

Domingo laughed at the shepherd's scolding. "Only
hasta la vista! Till we meet again, day after tomorrow.
Look, Juan, the flocks begin to move. Adios! To God!
Adios, Gaspar!"

"Adios, Señor," Juan flung back over his shoulder as
the tiny Rivera flock began to flow toward the plaza.

Already the soldiers were spurring their steeds out through the gate, and herders were urging their beasts to follow. While Old Juan trotted behind the Rivera sheep, young Gaspar rode ahead of them. Domingo quickened his stride to a run and within a few yards caught up with him.

"I wish my uncle could spare you something better to ride than that old gray rack of bones," Domingo sputtered boyishly.

Glancing gravely down at him, Gaspar made no reply. Even on this sway-backed, large-headed mount he rode proudly, almost haughtily. For two years he had been a slave in the household, yet he remained almost as aloof as the day when Uncle Melchior and Domingo fetched him home from the fair, where Don Melchior had bought him.

In tinkling unison the small flock trickled through the plaza amid the compact masses of men and sheep and goats and cattle that were crowding slowly toward the exit. As the leaders came abreast of the Indian house where the Riveras were quartered, Domingo dropped out of the throng. He could see better from an upstairs window.

Lightly he ran up the ladder and joined his mother, aunt and sister at the third-story windows. By this time the whole plaza was jammed, from the fronts of these tall adobe houses, built by the rebel Indians, across to the portales of the Governor's Palace.

Tina Nina was stretching up on her fat little tiptoes, to peer over the high sill, her soft chins resting on her dimpled fingers. "Ay de mi!" she murmured, clucking her disapproval as she looked down at some of her neighbors. "I always said Doña Ana was no lady. See how she struts in all that crowd, showing off her new shawl as bold as brass. And the fringes are as long as mine."

Doña Leonor smiled absently at her sister-in-law.

"See, Mother!" cried Lucia. "Old Juan has Tuson de Plata riding in style, as you ordered him to do."

Still distrait, Doña Leonor nodded. Domingo thought, with satisfaction, that his mother also recognized the importance of this hour. A new home—entirely new and fresh to Domingo—and who could foretell what excitement, adventure, prosperity? There would be nothing dull about resettling Santa Cruz!

The shouting, laughing, shrieking people; the bleating, braying, whinnying, squealing animals; the noise and color and eddying movement which pushed slowly toward the exit—these tugged the Rivera hearts after them.

They drew Domingo's thoughts away from the past nine months, when the five Riveras and Rosa and her daughters and their husbands and children, and Old Juan and Gaspar, all had been crowded into these few stark rooms. Behind those months, almost lost in the distance, lay the hard, slow miles from Mexico City, when snows had halted them and dust storms had buffeted them and blinded them; when they had sweltered and frozen and starved and grown dirty and sick with the endless march. Entirely lost in the far background were the Mexico City years, when they had hungered for their homeland; when Doña Leonor and Domingo and Lucia had longed passionately for a home of their own, instead of a corner in their uncle and aunt's house.

For Doña Leonor there were still earlier memories: the tragic recollection of stealthy flight and of their father's arrow wound and death; happy memories of what had gone before, their own estancia or hacienda, in the Valley of the Neighbors, their own flocks of sheep, which had increased, increased, and given the young family a sunny and spacious life. For Doña Leonor this day could not promise complete happiness, since Don José did not share it with her. For Domingo, who could not remember his father, it was without a shadow.

Looking from the window, Domingo could make out the red banda around Gaspar's head, moving out of sight and reappearing on the hilly road beyond the city wall. He could see the lumpy undulations of the seventy Rivera sheep, tawny white mottled with brown and black. He could see Old Juan's dwarfish body moving rhythmically behind them, beside Raton, the burro. And on the burro's back—

"Look!" Lucia sang out, as if she had just caught sight of it, too. "Look! Tuson de Plata himself!"

"Lucia, what is all this talk of Silver Fleeces?" Tia Nina inquired fretfully, easing herself down from her tiptoes. "You have it wrong; it is the Golden Fleece. The order of our Spanish nobles is the Order of the Golden Fleece."

"But ours is the Order of the Silver Fleece, tia mia. And yonder rides the noblest knight of them all."

"I am sure I hope you know what you are talking about," her aunt grumbled, retreating to the comfort of a cushion on the Indian bench that ran around the wall.

The other three remained at the window watching the exodus. The flocks disappeared as the cart road clambered downward between dark dwarf evergreens, and reappeared on an upflung slope. So they vanished and returned to sight, vanished and returned, while the tinkling and bleating and braying grew fainter, until at last the wayfarers were lost to eye and ear.

Then, presently, Old Rosa came puffing up the ladder with a basket of clean clothes on her head, clothes which had taken an extraordinary length of time to wash at the stream and dry on the bushes. Her daughter Soledad, slim and wide-eyed, silently followed, balancing another basket while children scampered before and behind. Lupe, Rosa's other daughter, came striding from the market place with food, her two-year-old Chiquita riding her hip along with a basket of vegetables. Nobody complained about the delay. Naturally the peones would wish to watch the departure of the flocks. It was a big hour.

It was a big hour. Day after tomorrow life would really begin. It might be hard for the Riveras, even now, to hold their own against the dark savagery of the land. It might take all their courage and wisdom and skill to keep Silver and his fellows from the clutching hands of preda-tory Indians. But it would be life, Domingo thought. It would be their own life.

Chapter 2

Homeward Bound

DAY after tomorrow came, though it had seemed to Domingo that it never would. It was April 21, 1695, the hour six in the morning, with birds twittering and the newly risen sun flooding the plaza with its rosy light.

The preceding day had been a race with time. Everything in the world had had to be done before the household wearily subsided to its rest. Yet now, at sunrise, there was still everything in the world to do.

The Riveras ate a sketchy breakfast, dropping down wherever they were, on the round-the-room bench or on the high hearth of a fireplace, and eating hurriedly. Uncle

Melchior was more approachable than usual. For weeks he had been like a bear with a sore paw. Doña Leonor said that men were naturally cross when they had to hang around the house, and especially a makeshift house, crowded and uncomfortable.

"Men are always excused for crossness and wildness and idleness," Lucia had muttered with a flash of the eyes at her brother. "It is only the women who are expected to be kind and gentle and sometimes, but not always, diligent."

This morning, however, Tio Melchior looked over his family with an unusual degree of indulgence as he blew on his chocolate to cool it, and munched a tortilla folded around well-seasoned meat.

"My dear, you look like a biscoche well stuck with raisins," he told his wife banteringly.

Domingo hid a smile. Tia Nina's hair, which she managed to keep very black, had retreated from her large forehead, so that it showed only from the sides and back. Without the waves to frame it, her whitely powdered round face looked larger and rounder.

Doña Leonor, on the other hand, was like a statue of the Lady of Sorrows. More specifically, she resembled the figure best beloved by General de Vargas: La Conquistadora, the Conquering Virgin. At the time of the Revolt, La Conquistadora had been rescued from Santa Fe, and in 1693, when De Vargas besieged and reconquered the capital, the Lady had ridden home triumphant. In gratitude for her aid and protection, he made a vow to build a chapel on the ground where his soldiers had encamped for the siege, and to carry La Conquistadora every autumn in victorious procession from that chapel to the big church in the Villa.

It was a beautiful little statue, more lifelike than most of the carved wood santos, and more regal. And Doña Leonor's face had a similar pure oval, her finely carved features the same high, sad dignity, her shadowed eyes the same blue.

"Lucita mia," Tio Melchior went on, his heavy-lidded gray eyes scrutinizing the girl satirically over his tilted cup, "I see you have also stuck your little face in the flour."

He drained the cup, wiped his mouth, and rose to give himself a leisurely survey in the one mirror that still hung in its place. Frowningly he brushed a smudge of whitewash from the shoulder of his fine leather jacket, a few crumbs from the broad white tabs of collar spread out over the leather in front. It was apparent that he found himself a handsome figure of a man, and Spanish from the steep forehead, hooded eyes and beaked nose, to the sheathed sword and roweled spurs.

The breakfast group broke up and went about its several affairs. Uncle Melchior departed. Doña Leonor went into the next room to oversee the work of Rosa and her daughters. Lucia set at packing the last freshly ironed clothes in a leather chest. Only Domingo, who always felt empty, and Tia Nina, went on eating.

Tia Nina's face drooped plaintively. She took another spoonful of the thick, spiced chocolate and moaned, "Mm, mm, mm," as she swallowed it; and then, in a soft whimper, "Raisins, indeed! My eyes have been praised more than once, Don Melchior! In a song contest. I well remember, they were likened to stars. And to capulines, dark, ripe choke-cherries. A biscoche indeed!" Broodingly she contemplated the actual sweet biscuit in her cushiony hand, took a bite from it, and murmured anew.

"It is a beautiful day, God be praised," Doña Leonor

observed, coming in briskly with another armload of clean clothes. "In this country the spring weather is something that cannot be relied on. But today—"

Lucia threw back her head and drew a sibilant breath, as if tasting the air that came through the windows. "But in here it is stifling hot," she complained.

"Thank heaven we shall not have to be crowded into these little boxes of rooms any longer," Tia Nina said aggrievedly.

It was as if she were thinking that the three other Riveras, Mother, Domingo and Lucia, had been the last straw, making the Indian house unbearable. She had a genius for saying the unpleasant thing.

Lucia frowned darkly in her direction. "You have put the Santo Niño where he will be safe, Mama?" she called, waiting on her knees with the lid of the rawhide chest still raised.

The figure of the Blessed Boy was the family's dearest treasure. It was tiny, not so long as Domingo's hand, cunningly fashioned of wood and jointed so that it could sit down. It had a chair to sit on, wrought of pure silver, and a little silver chest for its elaborate wardrobe.

Doña Leonor came to the doorway to answer. "Between the pillows, in the bottom of the other leather chest. And I warned him, kindly, of course, that it was to his interest to see that we came safely to Santa Cruz. If things should not go well, I would simply leave him in the chest awhile. He would not like that."

"If things should not go well?" Tia Nina echoed wailingly, holding out her emptied plate and cup to Rosa, and puckering her face like a baby. "Why must you frighten me so, Leonor? Is it not bad enough that we must leave Mexico City and come back into this wild country? Governor de Vargas should not have brought us if he could not keep us safe. I have never been the same woman since the Revolt. The terror of that year made an invalid of me." She pressed her dimpled hands piteously to the crumb-laden folds of her bodice.

"Now, now, Ninita," Doña Leonor comforted her, "the danger is slight, with thirty soldiers to escort us. Indian arrows make small headway when they try to pierce our men's leather jackets and shields. The Indians, on the other hand, possess nothing that can stop our powder and shot. Save a few who robbed our soldiers of their mail fifteen years ago. They might attempt to make off with a few of the slower horses, or with a cow or sheep or two from the stock that was sent on ahead. But they are not in the least likely to attack our company."

"A sheep or two?" Lucia cried anxiously. "Oh, Mama! I knew I should carry Silver in my arms."

"Hush," Doña Leonor said decisively. "Old Juan would guard that lamb with his life, and you know it well. Make haste, my child. Remember that this is one day when we dare not be late." Mother spoke without glancing at her sister-in-law, who was habitually tardy.

In the adjoining room, Old Rosa was sitting on her heels before the fireplace, dividing her time and attention between the tortillas baking on a copper sheet and the beans cooking in an earthenware pot. The migrants must have food to carry with them for the rest of the day.

"Roque!" Doña Leonor called. "Fernando!"

At her call, two small, dark mestizos came padding in on soft sandals from somewhere, wiping their little black mustaches with the backs of their hands. They were Rosa's sons-in-law. With smiling nods, they seized the chests Doña Leonor indicated, hoisted them to their

backs, and eased their headstraps round burden and forehead. Bent like half-open jackknives, they clambered down
the ladder.

The rooms emptied out until the feet of family and
servants and children, weaving a maze of busy steps through
them, had a different sound, an echoing, hollow sound.
And none too soon. Down in the plaza the people and
horses and oxen and burros and dogs and carts and hens
and roosters had worked themselves into a dizzy confusion,
a deafening clangor, as great as the babel of two days
earlier, though different.

Now the sweet shrillness of trumpets pierced it through
and through. Like a boiling kettle when a stream of cold
water is poured into it, the plaza fell quiet.

The Riveras crowded to their windows. This was a
sight to remember. Mexican women pattered backward in
a swirl of red petticoats, yanking their children out of the
way. Tlascalan Indian servants pressed against the house
walls, the men in white cotton shirts and breeches, the
women in petticoats and camisas. Cotton-clad Tanos Indians
stood straight and sullen in this place that had once been
theirs. A few Taos Indian men were among them, grim
statues, their cotton blankets thrown over their heads and
up across their left shoulders, like the Mexican women's
rebozos.

Patient oxen stood hitched to carretas piled with chests
and mattresses and here and there a carved chair. Burros,
with their drivers' coats over their heads, drooped fore
and aft. Without disturbing the enormous loads packed
on their backs mules swung nervous heels and cleared an
arc around them. Dogs wove in and out, yelping at a
mule's kick or at a nip from another dog or at the toe
of a soldier's boot. All this color and movement wove

a giddy pattern against the long, low portales of the Governor's Palace across the plaza, under the soft blue canopy of the April sky.

Close upon the fanfare of trumpets had followed the stately beat of horses' hoofs upon the packed earth of the square. Against the varicolored background, the animals loomed grandly, arch-necked and high-stepping, a-jingle with the load of iron pendants that fringed their skirtlike trappings.

Hats were snatched off. Hands fluttered like leaves, from forehead to left breast to right breast, making the sign of the cross. No wonder. High in the light, bright April air, held aloft by the standard-bearer, the banner of Our Lady and the Spanish Kingdom shone proudly in the sun, its satin rippling suavely, its gold tassels and gold leaf and gold embroidery gleaming. On one side of the great banner was blazoned Our Lady of Remedios, in a blue mantle and golden halo; on the other, the crests of Castile and Aragon. Hardly soiled, hardly tarnished by battles and journeyings, by blood and storm, the standard sailed triumphant. Under it the great general had ridden to the reconquest of the capital, and under it he would lead the settlers today, to found anew the city of Santa Cruz.

Proud and straight the General sat his horse. Today he felt secure enough to dispense with armor, though perhaps a vest of mail was concealed beneath his ruffled shirt. With the air of the Spanish grandee that he was, he wore his blue breeches, his plumed hat, his gold-cloth jacket with embroidered frills showering from the turned-back cuffs. His mustaches and small beard were pointed like stilettos, and his hair curled lightly on his shoulders. Domingo's heart leaped with admiration and love. With such a leader, and under such a banner, their journey was a crusade.

General de Vargas and the mounted military rode on across the plaza to the single gate of the city, and the migrating settlers began to draw in behind them in motley array. Upstairs in their dismantled rooms, the Rivera women snatched their shawls closer around them and made another hurried round of the apartment to be sure they had left nothing behind.

"Mi ojero, mi mas buen ojero!" Tia Nina was lamenting shrilly as she fluttered here and there, poking at abandoned debris in search of the small embroidered bag in which she carried the cornhusks for her cigarettes.

"You have it in your bodice, Ninita," Doña Leonor told her patiently. "Now follow Domingito down the ladder, so that he may steady you if you grow giddy. I will come behind."

Sighing and shaking and declaring that she would never again climb a ladder as long as she lived, Tia Nina wobbled down the almost vertical height. As soon as her aunt's weighty little body was safe on the ground, and her mother's smoothly moving one had joined it, Lucia ran down, the servants and the children following. They boosted Tia Nina into one of the carretas and established her on a wool-stuffed colchon, with a pillow at her back. Then Doña Leonor, Lucia and Old Rosa tucked themselves in amid chests and colchones.

Fernando, walking beside the two yoke of oxen, flicked them with his whip. The creatures heaved at the long cart tongue, the great discs that were the wheels turned with a mournful shriek, and the chariot of the Rivera ladies fell into line behind the mounted soldiers, with Don Melchior grandly astride his big black horse. Domingo rode just ahead of the carreta. His sleek steed, Cuero de Oro, Skin of Gold, was a beautiful creature, small but wiry, his tawny hide rippling over his muscles as the satin of the banner rippled in the breeze, his mane and tail glistening amber.

The Riveras' second carreta followed the first. It was well loaded, carrying not only Old Rosa's daughters, Lupe and Soledad, and their children, but also a squawking openwork crate of Castilian chickens. And besides these living creatures, it carried more colchones, more pillows, more chests, one carved cupboard with grillwork doors, kettles, kettle stands, earthen pots, wooden shovels and hoes, a few precious iron tools, plows with metal blades, all the scanty household gear which the Riveras had been able to cart up from Mexico City.

Out through the great gate in the city wall the horses went curveting. After them squalled the carretas, trotted the burros, trudged the foot passengers. Up and up the rising road they climbed.

Domingo twisted in his saddle to take one more look at the capital of the Kingdom of New Mexico. It was not much to see. Its buildings of adobe rose from the ground as if part of it. The string of low Royal Houses, joining the two- to four-story Tanos Indian ones, made a continuous structure round the main plaza. Only along the little Santa Fe River was the dusty bareness relieved by willows foaming with airy new golden-green leaves. Beyond the stream Domingo could see the shell of San Miguel chapel. It had been built for the use of the Tlascalan Indian servants whom the Spanish had brought up from Mexico. Now De Vargas was having it reroofed so that it could be put to general use, since the military chapel was too small and the Parroquia lay in ruins.

The emigrant train gradually strung itself out along the rolling hills, amid the endless reaches of twisted junipers and little piñon trees. Domingo and other riders wove in and out the length of the procession. The oxcarts lumbered steadily onward with their burdens, interspersed with and followed by a heterogeneous company. There were the pack mules and their drivers, the poorer householders bestriding burros, the very poor walking because they had no animals to ride. And among the foot travelers marched the infantry and trudged the missionaries, the Franciscan friars. Their cowled gray robes were girt up about their waists with a length of rope, and their sandaled feet patiently plodded through dust and stones.

Not for many years had so notable a concourse passed this way.

Chapter 3

The Creaking Miles

IN LUCIA, excitement was bubbling high. The air also bubbled, and the sunshine, and though there were few willows and plums in sight to bubble with new leaves, the fresh spring tips of the evergreens sparkled as gaily.

It was wonderful to be out and going somewhere. Tia Nina had been a virtual prisoner in Santa Fe, the fear of ladders her jailer. Only to attend Mass had she left her high cell, and then with groanings and quakings. Lucia had not been a captive, but neither had she been free. Naturally not, since she was a Spanish maid of fifteen, nearly sixteen, years, a ripe age for marriage. She had been almost as strictly chaperoned in Santa Fe as in Mexico City.

Mexico City had offered certain advantages that would be lacking in New Mexico. It was a big town, of perhaps twenty thousand inhabitants, with broad streets along which three great coaches could drive abreast. And while most if its houses were ground-hugging tiled adobes, it boasted grand mansions, too, and its rich Spaniards went resplendent in gold and jewels, in silks and velvets and brocades, in laces and plumes. It had also a university, founded in 1531; and games of chance; and bullfights; and dances.

The Riveras had taken small part in these splendors and gaieties. The great Pueblo Revolt impoverished them, and they lived in Mexico like exiles awaiting their return to the homeland. Though it was a homeland Domingo and Lucia could not remember, they were nevertheless familiar with the smallest details of the Rivera life there, for the family had talked of little else.

Their earliest American ancestors had come from Spain and up into Nuevo Mexico with Oñate, in 1598, when he founded the first capital, San Juan of the Gentlemen. Gradually they had established haciendas, estancias, ranchitos, near by, along the Chama and Santa Cruz rivers. Bringing sheep to a country avid for mutton and wool, they had prospered.

For some eighty years the Riveras had prospered. Though they must always be alert to the danger of Indians; though they must be content with primitive adaptations of the luxuries they had known in Mexico, they grew to love the new land passionately. It was theirs. They had hewed it out of the wilderness.

Don Melchior and Don José, the twins' uncle and father, were grandsons of the Rivera who came with Oñate. The two brothers grew up, married, and established their own ranchitos. Don José cultivated the fields and flocks with the wise skill of one who loves his calling. Don Melchior, more fiery and restless than his younger brother, had taken up soldiering, but his stock raising and farming were reasonably successful. He and Doña Nina were not blessed with children, and while Don José and Doña Leonor had several, they were snatched away by the diseases and accidents that killed so many frontier babies.

So when the twins were born, in 1679, and when they thrived, both families were beside themselves with joy. The children continued healthy and happy, even though they had to carry the names Domingo Roque Asuncion José y Maria Rivera y Baca, and Lucia Maria Eufelia Leonor Rivera y Baca. Nobody who was anybody could do without a grand parade of names.

For a time all had been pure sunshine for the Riveras. Then rose a tempest that wiped out their happiness and comfort.

The first Spanish settlers had found Pueblo Indians all up and down the valleys, living in tight towns—pueblos— and working their fields. The Spanish had taken over those early inhabitants, as subjects, willing or unwilling, of the King of Spain, and as converts to the Roman Catholic Church. In 1675 the conquerors hanged forty-seven of the Indian medicine men for stirring up rebellion. They severely punished many more.

Among the imprisoned medicine men was an outstanding Indian named Popé. As soon as Popé was released, he set about inciting his people to drive from New Mexico the three thousand Spanish settlers. He soon succeeded in rousing the tribes to such fury that they fell upon the Spanish and killed, burned and pillaged. The Riveras, except Don José, had been among those who escaped with their lives. Early in the flight from Santa Cruz he was mortally wounded by an Indian arrow, leaving his widow and children to his brother Melchior's care.

During the next few years Uncle Melchior had been a busy soldier, helping De Vargas put down the uprisings of the Mexican Indians. They too were loath to change their religion. They too disliked forced labor in building churches, as well as forced labor in Spanish mines. But at last De Vargas had subdued the rebels enough so that he could turn his attention to New Mexico. When word of the reconquest of Santa Fe reached Mexico City, the church bells shouted with joy, and the exiles hastened their preparations for return.

While Tio Melchior still held the papers of his original grant to the lands along the river, Doña Leonor's had been lost in the Revolt. The soldiers who were sent up to investigate conditions brought back word that livable buildings still stood on Don Melchior's ranchito, while Doña Leonor's had been destroyed and some of the materials used to erect an Indian watchtower.

It was still uncertain whether Doña Leonor could obtain a new grant to her old estancia; one of the soldiers had set his heart on having it, and had made petition for it; and since Doña Leonor could always have a good home with her brother-in-law, the authorities were inclined to give preference to the soldier. Doña Leonor was deeply anxious as to the outcome of her plea. The ranchito was a veritable sheep heaven, with mountainous land accessible for summer grazing, and lower meadows for the cold weather, with sunny south slopes where sheep flourished.

Although Tia Nina was now regretting the comfort and safety of Mexico City, she had during the years of exile unendingly pictured the charms of the lost home. And on the rare occasions when Lucia found her mother wiping away a tear, she knew that Doña Leonor was reliving the happy past. No wonder that the carreta could not move fast enough now for Lucia.

Soon, however, her happy eagerness was ruffled by a small sniff from behind her. When it persisted, she twisted around to find its source. Doña Leonor was silent, though her lowered lashes were wet and she fingered her rosary. The sniffles came from Tia Nina. She seldom wasted an opportunity to weep, and now she busily dabbed her pinkened nose and eyes with the edge of her shawl, to preserve her powder from the flood.

Impatiently Lucia's eyes passed over her aunt's face to rest on her mother's. "Mother mine," she begged, "why not be happy, when we are coming home?"

Doña Leonor smiled at her, winking away the tears. "The last time we passed over this road," she said; and stopped and began again. "The years seem to have slid away, and you and your brother—"

"Like two dolls," Tia Nina put in, as if regretting their growth. "And as sweet and beautiful as angels."

"And your father," Doña Leonor murmured. "Your dear father, may he rest in peace. It was just about here that he suffered his mortal wound. An Indian, shooting from a rock very like that one yonder—"

Lucia shivered, and scrutinized the rock for any hostile movement. But today, with the thirty soldiers, she reminded herself, it was absurd to feel this sudden fear quivering through her body.

"Mother mine, beloved," she coaxed, "now we start anew. And again our flocks shall be great, and the name of Rivera shall be great, and we shall smile once more."

"Seventy sheep," Doña Leonor mused, shaking her head. "So meager a beginning. And mere churros, scrawny and bare-bellied and thin-wooled. And Apaches and Navajos, yes, and Pueblos also, waiting their chance to snatch them away."

"A scant seventy, true, but with Old Juan to shepherd them!" Lucia reminded her buoyantly. "Who else could have bred up a lamb like Tuson de Plata? Who else could have kept the remnant of a flock alive throughout the Mexico City years? As to their being mere churros, all the better! What if our kings will not permit their fine-fleeced merinos to leave the Spanish borders? Old Juan swears that no pampered merino can take the punishment our churro can; nor is any so good a mother. Besides, no other mutton tastes so delicious, and no other wool is so good to spin with the stick spindle and weave on our loom."

"Yes, we may be thankful for Old Juan," Doña Leonor agreed, smiling faintly, though her voice was still thickened with sorrow. "Not for nothing did he walk the flocks to and fro in his youth, from the Castilian mountains to the plains, summer and winter. And never have I seen his equal at breeding up the flock, so that each year our beasts were a little larger, their fleeces a little heavier. I wonder whether there is anything left of that great flock which we abandoned. I wonder whether Maria is alive."

"Maria? But she was surely too old to be still alive!" Lucia exclaimed. If only she could get her mother over this bad time, and past the tumbled expanse of fantastically shaped rocks where her father had been wounded! She seized on any topic that might divert Doña Leonor from the distant sorrow now brought so close. "Surely she has died long since," she gabbled on.

"Not unless your mother also is an old, old lady," dryly observed Doña Leonor.

Tia Nina squeaked her indignant astonishment, her sister-in-law being twenty years younger than she. "Maria would be thirty-odd years, maybe. Certainly she might be living, but I would be willing to wager that the flock is long since dead."

"Why so?" asked Lucia, still scanning the uneasy landscape, shimmering under the high sun.

"Maria is an Indian, is she not? And Indians know good mutton when they see it."

"But when it comes to sheep," Doña Leonor objected, "the Navajo Apaches are not like the other wild tribes. They are more like the Pueblos. They do not consider the sheep merely as meat. They have a natural feeling for the flocks. Besides, Maria, in the year and a half she was with us, learned a great deal from Juan. And she loved the poor woollies."

"Hmph," commented Tia Nina, easing her soft bulk into a more comfortable position on the mattress. "It seems to me you used to claim that she also loved you and Don José and the twins."

"Especially Don José," Doña Leonor recalled. "It was like worship, the way she looked at him. I myself was at first astonished that she did not choose to come with us, when we fled to Mexico. Yet it was not so astonishing. Why should she wish to go so far away from her own tribe, where she might never see them again?"

It was always like this, thought Lucia. One had only to mention Maria to work up a stout argument. Whenever her name was uttered, Tio Melchior looked scornful, and Tia Nina complained of her faithlessness. Old Juan admitted that she had proved a better hand with the sheep

than any of his men, but he bristled with resentment that
the big flock had been left with her. Doña Leonor, though
she defended the Navajo woman, always looked a little
mournful, as if Maria had failed her in a time of need.

Maria's story was one of the most familiar of the tales
Lucia and Domingo had grown up on. Don José had
rescued her from a band of Apaches who had captured her,
a young, dark, vivid girl no older then than Lucia was now.
He might not have risked the perilous adventure if he
had not seen the baby she was carrying on a cradleboard.
The tiny, furry-headed boy was about the size of Don José's
twins, and the child's great, black, angry eyes and wizened
little yellow face gripped at Don José's kind heart.

He had brought them home, the girl and her little
son, and Old Rosa had given her a tremendous scrubbing
and put her into Mexican blouse and petticoats, while Doña
Leonor, cooing and crying out with pity, bathed the tiny,
skin-and-bones baby and gave him a sugar-tit to suck. El
pobrecito! she always said when she told the story, not
only was he half starved, but also crippled, one little leg
lying still and crumpled when the other drew itself up
and kicked out protestingly at a hard and bitter world.
The two Navajos were baptized and named Maria and
José, and Maria quickly learned to understand the Spanish
tongue. Occasionally she even spoke it.

"She was very-very smart, Maria," Doña Leonor said
now, as if her thoughts had walked the same path as Lucia's.

Tia Nina snorted. "Smart enough. But without gratitude."

"She was the first to tell us that she had heard that
the Pueblos were plotting revolt," Doña reminded her.
"Otherwise none of us might have reached even Santa
Cruz alive."

"Certainly she was well paid for anything she ever did

for us," Tia Nina retorted. "She took all those sheep, did she not?"

"We could not take them with us," Doña Leonor said reasonably. "Clogged with a great flock, we should all have been killed. I am sure I hope she got some good of them, and that they did not all go into the stomachs of Apaches and Comanches and wild beasts."

Doña Leonor's voice trailed off, her eyes dilating as she contemplated a great rock above the road. It resembled, Lucia thought, some strange recumbent animal, but to her mother it was doubtless only a reminder of past terror. Lucia waved and urgently beckoned to her brother, posting along the line of march, and he reined in beside the slower-moving carreta.

"Everything all right?" she asked, blinking a signal which said in their own code, *Talk to our mother. She is grieving again.*

Domingo spoke heartily, after a veiled glance at Doña Leonor. "All goes well. Not a hostile spear to be seen. Yonder to the west we could make out Tesuque Pueblo, though its mud houses hide themselves amid the rocks and the sagebrush. We could even distinguish Indians watching from the housetops, and with no sign of weapons. One or two, I am bound to say, were capering about as if to mock us."

"Are the Tesuques Friendlies or Unfriendlies?" Tia Nina quavered, her eyes rolling fearfully westward.

Domingo laughed. "Tesuque is very-very friendly, tia mia. Just now, when we have an escort of mounted and armed soldiers. But call them Friendlies or call them Unfriendlies, they are all much alike if ever they catch us napping."

Lucia felt a momentary chill, as if a cloud had covered

the sun. She shivered and snugged closer about her the
rebozo which up to now had been more useful as protection from the blazing sun. It was true that even the
quieter Pueblo Indians were not dependable. And they were
many, their towns stretching from far south in Rio Abajo—
Lower River—up to the Rio Arriba region, and the great
man-made mountain of Taos Pueblo. Their presence, their
potential strength, their resentment, formed the black
cloud that briefly hid her sun of happiness. And in addition there were other and more savage tribes hostile alike
to Pueblo Indians and to Spanish.

Reining in his mount, Domingo rode so close to the
carreta that Lucia could feel the warm breath from Oro's
star-blazoned golden nose when he whiffled with impatience
to be off. "Soon we come to Pojoaque Pueblo," Domingo
said.

"Pojoaque? Pojoaque?" Tia Nina stuttered anxiously.
"Are they Friendlies? Will it be a place to stop and have
the comida? I am faint from hunger, and my bones ache
with the racking of this cart."

Out ahead they could see Indians on the terraced flat
roofs of the adobe pueblo, their cotton blankets pale against
the deep blue of the undulating hills. Quickening its pace,
the train soon reached the outskirts of the village. As the
general and the officers turned their mounts inward between
the houses and the corrals and stables, a Franciscan padre
emerged with hands upraised in welcome, several Indians
at his heels.

"We shall have dinner," Tia Nina said hungrily.

Her companions were more concerned with the drama
of the scene. "Blessed be the Father, the Son, and the
Holy Virgin!" De Vargas called in a resonant voice.

"Forever!" shouted the Indians.

"And to think," Tia Nina twittered, "that fifteen years ago they burned the chapels and killed the blessed priests, those very same Indians."

Up ahead, De Vargas dismounted and dropped on one knee to receive the padre's blessing. The light glinted from the gold trimming of his hat as he swept it off, plumes floating. Soldiers jerked off their hat-helmets and followed their leader in doing reverence to the gray- cloaked friar, and some of the migrating settlers surged forward and joined them.

The Pojoaque priest leading the way, the officers and Franciscans from the caravan strode into the convent. Soon afterwards Indians emerged, bearing pottery jars that steamed with the heartening fragrance of chocolate and baskets of gray bread as thin as tissue. Under the high, warm sun the train relaxed into a picnic party. Settling back solidly, the oxen blew a little and rested from the long pull, for even an empty carreta was a monstrous load, its frame, axle, tongue, made from ponderous tree trunks, and each splint of its basketlike body a smaller log.

Old Rosa's crew of grandchildren ran to and fro, while their grandmother shouted warnings of the mules' heels and of strange dogs and of rattlesnakes. The little things were wild with freedom, pulling wisps of grama grass and saltbush to feed the oxen, and pushing each other about joyously.

Old Rosa and her daughters were soon serving their masters and mistresses a picnic repast of tortillas and peppery frijoles. Munching her tortilla, which was folded around a ladleful of the beans, Lucia scrambled from the carreta and walked back along the train, Domingo sauntering at her side. Since most of the company had shared the arduous journey from Mexico City, as well as the later months in

Santa Fe, they had become almost like one large household. Other families, from other parts of Mexico, had migrated ahead of them. Still others had come later, and had been crowded into the Royal Houses and the Tanos dwellings as best they could be. Father Farfan's sixty-six and a half families had been forced into greater intimacy by the strangeness of some of these resettlers, at whom Tia Nina, especially, looked down her nose. Their own group, Tia Nina boasted, was the only one selected for its quality.

It must be admitted that the Farfan caravan was made up of respectable people, even though most of them were now impoverished, and many of a Spanish lineage less pure than Tia Nina claimed. On the other hand, some of the bands of resettlers had been recruited from the jails of Old Mexico, and others from among peons working in the mines.

Now Lucia spoke politely to the women—"Como está Usted, Doña Eufemia? Como está Usted, Doña Ana?"— and called gaily to the girls, and avoided the persistent eyes of Salvador, and accepted coolly the bunch of blue larkspur offered by Higinio Padilla, mincing and bowing. She disliked the tall, thin pallid youth even more than she did Doña Ana's Salvador. In order to dismiss him, she stopped beside the second of the Rivera carretas and engaged its occupants in talk. Soledad, always shy and fearful, had kept her youngest child in the cart with her when the others clambered out. Now the two-year-old Ramon held out his hands for Lucia to take him. Lucia swung the child to her hip and carried him to Doña Leonor.

"Did you see the antelopes we scared up back yonder?" Domingo asked. "There they were, all facing our way and with their ears pricked up—as curious as a girl," he added teasingly. "I could easily have brought one down, only General De Vargas gave orders that there was to be no hunting on this trip. So I waved my arm at the criaturas, and before you could blink there were white rumps where the big eyes had been and—puff!—they were gone like thistledown. Ah, look! Señor De Vargas comes out of the pueblo."

De Vargas advanced, delicately wiping his lips with a white handkerchief, glancing at the high sun, tugging his fat watch from his girdle. In a moment he was again in his saddle, setting spur to his mount. Once more the train spun out behind him, the Spanish children running breathlessly back to their mothers, and waving at scantily clad Pojoaque children on the housetops.

On and on creaked the carreta, up the little hills and down the little hills, over sandy wastes, between the eternal piñons and junipers, amid the rounded clumps of gray sage, which gave back to bruising hoofs and wheels a hot, bittersweet pungence. Soledad's little Ramon began to fuss in his dusty weariness, and Lucia lifted him from Doña Leonor's lap and cradled him in her own while she told him a favorite story—"Una paloma vivia en el monte." By the time she had dramatically repeated the mother dove's cry to the coyote—"No, I will not give you my baby!"—Ramon was fast asleep, raspberry red mouth open and long black lashes shadowing his red-brown cheeks. Tia Nina also was drowsing, her double chins resting so cozily on her cushiony bodice as almost to strangle her rich snores.

By now everyone was tired of riding. Doña Leonor and Lucia shifted their numb bodies on the folded mattresses, momentarily relieving the achy stiffness. Old Rosa, complaining under her breath when the heavy carreta

jounced mercilessly over a rock, or when a stretch of deep
dust sent a smothering cloud into the faces of the travelers,
lifted Ramon from her señorita's cramped arms. Children
clambered out of carts to run beside the trail and pick
spring flowers. Now and then they found a clump of
anemones that had stretched their furry necks longer and
longer as they grew old; or larkspur, or mertensia, or
starry white sand lilies which lost all their fresh sweetness
when the eager little hands grubbed up their stemless
calyxes.

Domingo's voice at length roused Lucia from a jolting
half-doze. "Yonder is San Cristobal Pueblo."

Pulling open heavy eyes, she blinked in the direction he
indicated.

"General De Vargas will pause here only long enough
to greet the padre who is in charge," Domingo spoke
softly, so as not to waken his aunt, "and to allow certain
letters and supplies to be left. The pueblo simmers with
discontent, Tio Melchior says. The General has permitted the Indians to remain until October, so that they
might harvest their crops, yet they are still sullen."

The sleep dropped away from Lucia's eyes as she stared
at the terraced adobe houses and the brush shelters. The
usual sentries stood straight and motionless, and there were
no waving hands, no welcoming shouts, but only the stiff
stillness of hate, of peace maintained by fear alone. Lucia
was glad when the train left behind the gaunt grayness
of the village.

The sun had long passed its zenith and was dropping
toward the western mountains, lower and lower until the
sky began to flame. To the right, eastward, towered
the snowy Truchas Peaks, and farther away, to the left, the
white summits of the Jemez Mountains. Now sunset color

began to tinge the snow; began to run along the weary train of oxen and horses and mules and burros and people. The lower mountains melted in rosy flame, and the peaks were as pink as heavenly peach blossoms.

"God grants us a good omen," Doña Leonor murmured through Tia Nina's sonorous sleep. "He lights our way as we approach our new home."

Lucia cried out at that. "Approach? Do we approach the New Town? But Old Juan and the flock! But Gaspar! But my little Silver! Where can they be? Could they have traveled so fast as to reach Santa Cruz before us?"

Tia Nina's snore exploded and she blinked open half-seeing eyes and groaned. Domingo made no reply to his sister's expostulation. His narrowed eyes were peering out under his hat brim. Suddenly he snatched off the hat and waved it jubilantly.

"Speak of the angels!" he cried, laughing down at his sister. "Yonder is Gaspar. And the angel flock also, as I live."

Lucia jumped up, falling over her sleep-numb feet. shading her eyes with her hand, she gazed forward where the head of the cavalcade was entering upon a level valley folded in between long lines of gentle hills.

There, in truth, she could make out the yellow-white mass of the sheep, and Gaspar, erect upon his bony gray mount, and Old Juan, standing small beside the burro Mouse, as he watched his milling flock. Lucia could even see, protruding from one of the Mouse's saddlebags, a dab of white that could be nothing less than the lamb Silver.

"The angel Plata! Now God be praised!" she breathed.

All was well with Lucia's world.

Chapter 4

A Dream Come True?

THE proudly stepping vanguard halted. The rear of the caravan quickened its pace. The whole motley throng had soon telescoped there before the walled town of Santa Cruz. Another great moment had arrived; another gaily colored pageant was about to be enacted.

Not yet could Domingo see the New Town as a small, stark village, as the Indian pueblo it had become since 1680. Recalling their entry later, he thought that the mean little mud villa had been like an ugly woman disguised by a rainbow of veils and by the swing and swirl of the dance. Santa Cruz was transfigured by the joyously

42

milling throng, the gay diversity of people and costumes, the renewed clamor, the thrill of reaching at last the goal toward which they had all been endlessly toiling. Even the cloud of dust raised by the crowd was gilded by the setting sun, so that the hollow square of tall houses floated in light, and their long ladders rose out of a shining cloud.

In true Spanish style, the General had planned the entry beforehand, and now he allowed no loitering. To have the desired solemnity and splendor for his travel-worn, hungry people, the formal occupation of the New Town must be carried out with snap and speed. Drama meant much to the leader, and as much to his followers, since they also were of Spanish blood. Time enough to think of food and lodging when the pomp of pageantry was past.

Again there was a space of laughter and confusion, while, just inside the gate, De Vargas sat his mount and watched with mingled impatience and tolerance. Two fierce Spanish sheep dogs fell to fighting in the midst of the throng, and growls, snarls, yelps, shouts and the crack of whips rose above the sea of sound. Babies woke as they were lifted out of carretas, and their howls were jounced into hiccuppy quiet or suddenly smothered with food. And, as before, the tumult was gradually shaken down into a semblance of order.

Leaving their horses with servants, the mounted soldiers joined the general in the plaza, foot soldiers and heads of families following them. There, near the little chapel, they drew up in a semicircle that curved out grandly from De Vargas at its center, while behind them, tiptoe in the carretas or peering between the men, were the women and children and servants.

Domingo stood very straight. At fifteen, one was nor-mally half-man and half-boy, but as head of his house

Domingo was three-quarters man. Or he would be, if ever they could get into a hacienda of their own.

All this ceremonial pageantry was helping to bring nearer the glad day.

De Vargas was speaking. He was administering the oath of office to the new town officials and to a few others in the semicircle: the alcalde mayor, the war captain, the lieutenant and his ensign, the squad corporals. Nine or ten soldiers were to be stationed here, since this was the farthest frontier.

As Domingo watched the officials, hats off, step forward a pace from the line, icy fingers played along his spine and to the crown of his head.

The solemn, ringing voice of De Vargas as he issued the oath stilled the last murmurous rustle. These men were to accept for their fellow townsmen and themselves this place and its environs, *La Nueva Villa de la Santa Cruz de los Mejicanos Españoles del Rey Nuestro Señor Don Carlos Segundo*—the New Town of the Holy Cross of the Spanish Mexicans of the King Our Lord Don Carlos the Second. As loyal subjects, they must maintain and preserve it, even at the expense of their own lives. When they had taken the oath, Governor De Vargas once more made declaration of the grant, conferring likewise posses-sion of all minerals in the Chimayó Mountains.

Domingo's eyes widened. From the time when Coronado came seeking treasure here a hundred and fifty years ago, there had been dazzling stories of New Mexico's gold and silver and turquoise. Gold!

As if in harmony with his thoughts, the sky deepened its radiance. From bright cloud billows flecks of pure fire sailed out into the pale blue. As Governor De Vargas turned to the Franciscan friar at his side, the sky above the chapel poured out a flood of golden light. Domingo crossed himself. Was not this a holy promise?

Still illumined by the sky, De Vargas took Fray Antonio Moreno's hand with courtly deference and led him into the chapel, to which Father Francisco De Vargas, custodian of the region, had appointed him, and bestowed on him possession and full direction of it. From that moment Fray Antonio was Chaplain of Santa Cruz.

The ceremonies were almost over. The alferez unsheathed his sword and swore to possess and defend the new settlement, and after that all present shouted as they were bidden, "Long live the King our Lord, whom may God preserve, the Señor Don Carlos the Second, King of the Spaniards."

Domingo's neck was stiff with excitement, and with standing so straight and still. It was a relief to cheer with all his might, to let loose the exaltation that had swelled within him. He too would serve the King, and the cross, and protect his mother, his sister, and his flock.

The first shout was like a rehearsal, feeble and scattering, but the next was steady and full-throated. Hats were jubilantly tossed in air, and the fringe of women, children and servants joined the chorus. The third pæan was deafening, redoubled as it was by the echoing square of adobe walls. Through its clamor, Domingo caught the thready sweetness of his sister's voice, only a few feet away. Nor was that all: following it like the last word in a sentence came a tremulous "maa-aa"!

Domingo's head jerked round, eyes shocked and questioning. Between the shoulders of two women he could see Lucia's face, rosy, but not with remorse. She was pressing the nose of the struggling, kicking Plata into her neck to muffle his bleating. Blackly Domingo scowled at her. Then, to his vast relief, the villa shook with a salute of gunfire. Before its roar ceased ricocheting from one side of the plaza to the other, it was succeeded by a second and a third. All thoughts of irreverent sister and lamb were beaten out of Domingo's mind by the rattle and bellow and bang.

That night the whole caravan camped within the walls of Santa Cruz. Everyone found at least temporary lodging in the houses the Tanos Indians had built for themselves and reluctantly vacated at the General's order. In the flickering light of the cedar-bark torches, Doña Leonor and Doña Nina dubiously inspected the quarters assigned to them. Rosa and her daughters opened out the mattresses and spread them with serapes. The Riveras might sleep more comfortably if they kept on their clothes tonight. They were all tired from the journey, and, as soon as they had eaten a sketchy meal of tortillas and beans, they dropped blessedly to sleep.

With the dawn the new villa was astir. The people were eager to claim their houses, clean and whitewash them, and settle in. No less eager were the Riveras to get out to Tio Melchior's rancho and discover what was needed to make its dwellings livable.

In the early morning light some glamour still veiled the stark village of Santa Cruz, but as the sun rode higher, it revealed all its dusty bareness. Domingo caught his sister at the window, staring wide-eyed at plaza and buildings.

"My soul and body, little sister," he murmured, "you look almost as badly taken aback as Tia Nina."

"But—did you suppose it would be like—like this?"

Her expression was so doleful and deflated that he laughed aloud. "Come now, Señorita!" he teased her. "Surely you were not expecting another Mexico City! Santa Fe gave you a bad jolt too; remember? We knew that Santa Cruz was nothing more than an outpost in the Indian country. How could it equal even Santa Fe, then, the capital of the kingdom?"

His sister sniffed delicately, drawing up her eyebrows, blinking her misty eyes clear, drawing down her upper lip, and sniffing again. Domingo always watched her short nose when she went through this routine. Whenever her other features moved, the tip of her nose drew in quaintly. And whenever she looked at him like this, with wide, wet eyes that refused to admit their wetness, he felt much older than his twin, and large and strong and protective.

"Sister, I am not at all disappointed," he assured her. "Already I like it better than Mexico City. Here we shall have room; we shall have freedom."

Lucia giggled, perhaps because her brother was standing so straight that he bent backward, puffing out his chest like a pigeon, and pounding it with his fists. He did not mind her laughter. He was too much exhilarated by the light, keen air, sharpened with the smoke of juniper and piñon burning in the ovens and fireplaces. It was really going to be a grand new life, he thought exultantly.

"Besides," put in Lucia, still gazing doubtfully from the window, "Mother and Tia Nina have always bragged more of their ranchos than of the villa. I can hardly wait to see the estancia."

Their mother paused behind them and joined the conversation. "It is as if we had been on a long journey—near fifteen years long. Only now are we ready to get down to the real business of living again."

Poor, poor Mother. Only ready to begin living again now when her life was practically done. Thirty-five years old, Doña Leonor was.

Breakfast over, the women and the servants climbed into

the carretas to ride out to the hacienda, Uncle Melchior and Domingo cantering ahead, Gaspar following with Old Juan and the flock. Before the morning meal Fray Antonio had celebrated the Mass, and Tia Nina was still ecstatically discussing him.

"He is beautiful, that padre, beautiful!" she gurgled, rolling up her eyes and clasping her dimpled baby hands. "He resembles nothing so much as the statues of El Cristo, so kind, so gentle, so holy, and with the golden hair like a halo, no less."

"Red hair, I call it," growled Uncle Melchior. "And in spite of the color, he is too gentle and kind by half. The frontier is no place for softness. These Pueblo Indians can be plotting to drive a spear into your heart, even when they look as harmless as so many sheep. Men of iron are needed here, in the church as well as among the military."

Again Tia Nina had spent an hour powdering her large round face, arranging her scanty black hair, and winding her rebozo just so, with the drape which indicated her status as wife. As the carreta jolted them over the winding road south and east of Santa Cruz toward the ranchito so long lost to them, she bounced with excitement as if she were riding to a grand ball.

"Do not expect too much!" Domingo warned his sister and aunt, reining his horse back beside the cart. "Remember Santa Cruz!"

Lucia spoke uncertainly. "The report was that Tio Melchior's houses were all standing, though ours did not fare so well."

"Even a wreck can stand, provided it has something to lean against," answered Domingo.

Nevertheless, Domingo himself held a mental picture of lofty walls with blue-painted gates and a gracious red glint of tiled roofs. In spite of his reason, he envisioned a patio with well-tended walks and shrubbery and flowers, and a small walled garden.

Now his mind was jerked into the present, into reality. Ahead of them, beside a crumbling adobe wall that was no more than a ridge of mud, Don Melchior had drawn up with a flourish that made his black mount shake its head and paw the air.

"Wh-what is it? What is it?" Doña Nina gabbled in alarm as the carreta squalled up to him. "Not Indians, Don Melchior? Not wolves? Not rattlesnakes, my beloved?"

Tio Melchior snorted. "Certainly not. Would I be sitting here like a wooden image if it were? It is your house."

"My house!" shrieked Doña Nina. "Oh, no, Don Melchior, not that ruin. Do not make a mock of me!"

"Ruin? This is no ruin!" her husband assured her indignantly. "This wall needs rebuilding, to be sure, but most of the casa stands firm and sound. Enter."

The first carreta screeched and squalled through the gateway, now a ragged breach, Don Melchior and Domingo falling in behind. The second carreta, with Old Rosa's daughters and their families, trailed by Juan and Gaspar and the flock, lumbered along to the next gateway, which led into the servants' courtyard. Once within the patio, Domingo drew a sharp breath and his aunt began to whimper disconsolately. Domingo looked at his mother. Doña Leonor did not appear in the least disappointed. With eyes shining through tears, she was gazing tenderly about her.

Domingo turned to look again, but still he saw only an angular *U* of one-story adobe rooms around a barren patio.

Lucia uttered a soft squeak, and he saw her nose twitch in as she raised her eyebrows and blinked her eyes, twitch again as she drew down her mouth and sniffed. But once she had conquered the threatening tears she sparkled with gaiety and seemed to forget that she had ever felt like weeping.

"Tia Nina, we can paint the house fronts blue, no?" she cried eagerly. "Sky blue. We can plant—pronto!—the flower seeds we have fetched. And will it not be wonderful to be living once again where we have space enough to turn ourselves about?"

Domingo chuckled. He never knew what to expect of this twin of his. He himself was good at thinking, but Lucia was better at accomplishing. Often she began to act on his ideas before he had finished expressing them.

Chapter 5

The Padre

TIO MELCHIOR dismounted, shouting to Roque to take his horse, and strode over to the well in the center of the courtyard.

"Viva!" His voice echoed hollowly from the depth as he peered down. "Only a little repair and a big cleaning, and we have our good water."

Lucia jumped to the ground and reached up a hand to Doña Leonor. With Rosa's support and encouragement, Tia Nina clambered out, a jelly of wheezing sighs and cries and oozing tears. As soon as she had her mistress safe on her inadequate little feet, Old Rosa lumbered off across the patio and disappeared through an arched passageway into the service court. A minute or two later she waddled breath-lessly back, her broad, dark face beaming.

"Now God be praised!" she cried. "At once I can bake fresh biscoches. There stands my oven, quite as I remem-bered it: my small oven, the best I have ever used."

Tia Nina, cheered by the mention of biscoches, was tod-dling toward one of the many doors that opened on the patio. Doña Leonor and Lucia, Don Melchior and Domingo, fol-lowed her. The long room they entered was dimly lighted, sunshine filtering through sheets of mica in the high win-dows.

Tia Nina's face was doleful again. "Completely empty," she faltered. "Not a stick of furniture left."

"What did you expect, woman?" Tio Melchior retorted impatiently.

"The windows are all whole," Doña Leonor reminded her. "At least in this sala. These rooms they have evidently used, the Indians have."

"Madre," Domingo dropped on one knee as he presented himself to his mother, "by your leave I will follow Old Juan and Gaspar and see to the sheep."

She smiled at him mistily, and as he kissed her hand good-by, she turned it to pat his cheek. "Remember that this is wild country, my son. Remember how much you mean to your mother, and have a care. Go with God."

Bowing to his aunt and uncle as he went, Domingo backed out of the sala. Once outside, he went dashing through the gaping gateway and followed the trail of the sheep. Even if they had been much farther ahead he could have followed them, for their little cloven hoofs had marked the dust in a close-set pattern. He was soon abreast of Juan and Gaspar and Chepe, the puppy, gamboling along with Silver, the lamb.

"Those two think that they are brothers," Domingo remarked to Gaspar, laughing as the puppy rolled under the lamb's fleecy body and among his long legs, tumbling over and over and growling a baby invitation to play. Before Chepe's eyes were open, Old Juan had taken him from his mother and given him to Plata's mother to be nursed, as was the custom. Plata's twin had died, and Juan had tied its pelt securely on Chepe's little body, so that the ewe would smell it and identify him as her own. The woolly hide was by this time worn out, like a constantly used garment, and only a few strings of it still encircled Chepe's fluffy neck in a ragged collar. There was no longer any need of deception, for Plata's mother had fully accepted him as her son.

"He will make a fine sheep dog, that one," Old Juan said. "Before the flock begins to grow large I shall have in Chepe a better helper than Gaspar."

"This morning," Domingo said eagerly, "I go to the New Town to ask Fray Antonio whether the mission flock is yet big enough so that I—so that my mother—may purchase a few head immediately. A lay brother has been living in the convent and tending the sheep that were sent up earlier this spring."

"Did my lady give you permission?" asked Juan.

Domingo grew hot. Old Juan would never admit his maturity. "Yes," he answered stiffly.

Juan's mouth quirked and his deep-set eyes rolled impishly. "What think you of this grazing ground, master?" he inquired with mock humility.

Domingo spoke severely. "Fair. Only fair. Was my father's pasture land much better? Or is that another of the legends that have grown up in the minds of my elders during the years of absence? Santa Fe, the big, bustling capital of the kingdom! The beautiful villa of Santa Cruz!

Tio Melchior's grand casa! I find it very-very funny. And
the grazing land on which our flocks grew sleek and full-
fleeced! I suppose we shall find that rich pasturage as sparse
and weedy as this."

"Very fine forage it was," Old Juan assured him. "I, Juan
Padilla, I grow up as a pastor and the son of a pastor, in old
Spain, as you know." Domingo nodded impatiently. A
thousand times he had heard the fact. "Yet as I drove the
flocks on the long migrations from winter pasture to summer
and back again, never have I seen better browse than the
grasses and shrubs on the hacienda of your father, God rest
him. It is as if the vegetation in this dry land stores more
juices in the summer and holds them more securely in the
winter."

Domingo's expression disparaged the scanty pasture
around them, and he shrugged. "Weedy," he repeated.

"Do not make light of the weeds," Juan scolded. "Fresh
spring weeds are to the sheep's taste, and they fatten on them.
Plenty of mustard here, you may note, and of yarrow. Both
serve the flock for appetizer, for meal and for medicine.
Nor is there enough larkspur or whorled milkweed to im-
peril them."

Still Domingo looked unimpressed.

"Come then, my fine young gentleman," Old Juan said
sharply. "The hacienda that was your sainted father's is
only a stone's throw away. Though it is hidden by yonder
rise of ground, you can see the top of the tower which the
Tanos built upon it." He pointed with the angled throwing
stick he always carried. "You shall observe for yourself.
Though it is true that there has been much drought. There
was drought also in the years before the Revolt." He snorted
at the memory. "That heathen sorcerer, Popé, made the
Pueblos believe that it was the fault of us Spanish that the

skies were closed against the land. He told them that the Indian gods would give them abundance of rain, once they drove out the intruding Spanish."

Silver and two other early lambs had bounced ahead of the flock, Chepe yelping after them on his short legs. Like an India rubber ball Silver sprang upon an inviting rock, and poised there till one of his companions leaped to his side. Then he braced himself and briskly butted off the interloper. It was a game that Domingo had often watched and laughed at.

Walking slowly with the leisurely sheep, the man and the boys surmounted the rise and gazed across the savage little chasm of an arroyo. "The boundary between your father's old estancia and your uncle's," said Juan. "Up in yonder Truchas Mountains, out of which our blessed river comes frolicking, is the finest summer pasture one could ask, and only a day's journey for the flock. And over yonder rise"— his throwing stick pointed out a line of low hills—"is the perfect wintering ground, with a south slope and a natural corral. If only your lady mother can recover this grant—"

"We must," declared Domingo. "We will. It is really our own; and the Governor has showed himself just in such matters. I do not see why it was our buildings the Indians had to destroy, instead of my uncle's," he added frankly, his dark brows flying up in a *V*, as Lucia's were wont to do.

Out of his habitual silence, Gaspar spoke. "They build good tower. Like towers of the Old People." He tossed his head sidewise to indicate the wild desert to the north.

His eyes on the tower, Domingo dashed recklessly down the bank of the arroyo, stumbling and catching himself with difficulty. Gaspar followed lithely, and the two climbed the farther bank, pulling themselves up by rocky handholds, till they gained the grassy slope beyond.

"Juan, there have been sheep here," Domingo called back, dusting off his hands.

"De cierto," Juan responded. "The Rivera flock."

"Do you think I mean fifteen years ago? Lately. Maybe yesterday."

Old Juan grunted his surprised disbelief. With a puzzled shake of the head, Domingo raced on with Gaspar to the foot of the tower, a rounded structure with loopholes in the ramparts at its top, and windows below them. Suddenly Gaspar stopped and stared downward.

"What do you see?" demanded Domingo.

Gaspar shot out his lips in the Indian gesture of pointing. Against the foundation of the tower stood a small cairn of stones, with a bundle of rudely shaped sticks protruding from its top.

"Caramba!" Domingo spat out the word. "Some of the devilish work of Pueblo sorcerers, no, Gaspar?"

Gaspar made no reply.

Domingo wheeled round and scrambled down the arroyo again, his flesh crawling. Juan and Rosa—yes, and Tia Nina no less—were cram full of witch stories, both Indian and Spanish. Like all his family and neighbors, Domingo had grown up on such tales. He had seen people sicken and die upon learning that they were bewitched. In their baby-hood, he and Lucia had worn coral wristlets to ward off the evil eye and other harmful magic. Doña Leonor was seldom without her coral necklace, loving it not only for its color and carving, but for the sense of protection it gave her.

"I must hasten to inform Fray Antonio of this mischief," Domingo muttered, when he was across the chasm and at a safe distance from the tower. "He will take care of the business. Gaspar, we will go at once, and waste no time. You will not be needing our help, Juan?"

Juan's response was all his own, something between a laugh and a snort from behind pursed lips. "I?" he demanded. "I, who with trained sheep dogs have handled a thousand sheep?"

Doña Leonor had always said that the little old Spaniard was worth any three other men. He was a wizard with the slingshot, able, with a well-placed stone from it, to halt the headlong flight of the flock, or to cripple a predatory bird or beast. He was skilful also with the throwing stick, which the first Spanish had borrowed from the Pueblo Indians hereabout. Old Juan could send this boomerang skimming the ground like a live thing along the edge of the flock to turn its course of march whatever way he willed.

"Need you?" Old Juan repeated, even his fanlike ears quivering with amusement. "Go, young master, go!"

The two boys slid sheepish glances at each other, Juan's tone so flatly reduced them from their new maturity. Without more words, they went loping back to the hacienda, Domingo's vanity pricked anew by Gaspar's easy superiority in running.

In the home portal Domingo stopped short, surveying in alarm the bustling confusion indoors. At the same instant his mother caught sight of the boys, and her slightly abstracted eyes leaped to find something at which she could set them to work.

"Let us go and confer with the padre at once," Domingo murmured to Gaspar, moving quickly backward. "We shall be doing the women a favor by keeping out of their way."

With a glance of full understanding at each other, they slipped out of range. Oro and the gray were cropping grass round the edge of the patio. The two boys sprang to saddle and cantered through the wrecked gateway and west and north the quarter mile to Santa Cruz. Dismounting in the

plaza, they secured their horses and went to the door of the
convento, behind the chapel. There they halted to watch
and listen.

Lined up on hand-hewn log benches sat a score or more of
children. There were the children of the settlers and of their
servants, the little girls in red petticoats and camisas, the
little boys in shirts and tight trousers. And there were besides a scant handful of Tano Indian youngsters, perched
like birds about to take flight, clothed in shirts or dresses of
unbleached cotton. The Indian children's bare brown toes
curled and uncurled on the earthen floor or dangled above it,
and their eyes clung, fascinated, to the padre's face, while
they chanted after him the Spanish words of the catechism,
or uncomprehendingly moved their lips in unison with their
schoolmates.

Domingo thought that the room was like a picture painted
mostly in blacks and grays and whites, slashed with the red
of the petticoats. Fray Antonio in his rough rope-girdled
robe was a gray candle. The light from a translucent window
behind him, falling upon his head, kindled to flame the
fringe of hair around his tonsured crown. The pictures and
statues of the saints in their wall niches, and the handmade
flowers that decked these shrines, added further strokes of
color.

Fray Antonio smiled at the boys and nodded them toward
the rear benches. There they sat down to look and listen
until the padre dismissed his class and came forward to greet
them. At his approach, Domingo rose quickly and dropped
on one knee to receive his blessing. After a moment's hesi-
tation, Gaspar followed his example.

"You are not a Pueblo?" Fray Antonio observed, his
eyes searching Gaspar's face.

"No, Señor Padre. Dinneh."

"Ah, Apache de Navahu," the padre assented. "And you have been baptized into Holy Church?"

"Si, Señor."

"He was baptized at once, as soon as my uncle bought him," Domingo put in. "Two or more years ago it was."

The priest's eyes clouded as they rested on the livid scar that marred the Indian youth's forehead. Domingo slid a sidewise glance at it. He had gone into a tantrum of tears and stamping feet when his uncle had the fourteen-year-old slave branded. It was not the indignity but the physical hurt that outraged him. Branding was, after all, the custom, even though the priest looked as if it was a custom that he could not accept.

Domingo hastened to draw the padre's attention from the branded brow. "Padre, my mother, Doña Leonor, asked me to inquire whether the mission has any sheep to sell."

Fray Antonio blinked thoughtfully, shaking his head. "I will show you the mission flock," he offered, and led the way outdoors, girding up his gown and stepping sturdily on his sandaled feet. "You can see for yourself and explain to your lady mother that we have not yet reached the point where we can advantageously divide the sheep. My predecessor did well in the months that he spent here, but some of the creatures have had to become mutton to feed the convent, and the flock is only beginning to increase."

Herded by a Tano Indian, the woolly animals were grazing not far from the walls of the villa. "Buenas días, Marco," the priest greeted the herder. "We inspect your charges. Soon the lambs will come, no?"

"Si," the Indian answered, folding his lips on the word as if unwilling to let another escape. Domingo thought uneasily that these Tanos who had stayed behind and hired out to the settlers were a surly lot.

The flock was indeed small, and it was by no means so well bred up as Old Juan's. These, too, were the common Spanish churros, thin, leggy beasts, with loose wool of many colors. Here and there a ram belligerently surveyed the men from under a quaint cap of two to six curved horns. A few lambs bounded around their mothers.

"Our Pueblo Indians are as much at home with the sheep as if they had always had them." The padre smiled benignantly at the flock and at the equally responsive herder. "So also with your people, my son," he said to Gaspar. "They take to the sheep in both senses of the word. We teach the Pueblos, and they learn quickly. And then the Apaches de Navahu take from the Pueblos both the learning and the sheep." His mouth twitched into a smile at his own humor.

The tribe, small branch of the Apaches though it was, seemed to be here, there, and everywhere. Domingo had heard his uncle say that some Navajos sided with the Pueblos in their revolt against the Spanish, and then turned about and raided their allies, helping themselves to sheep and horses freely, to wives, and to children whom they could bring up as members of their own tribe.

"Father," said Domingo, as they turned back toward the convent, "I and Gaspar, we go today with Old Juan, our herder, to see the hacienda which was my father's, the one where they have built a tower out of the ruins of the house. And at the base of that tower we find sorcery."

The padre's brow furrowed, and the laughter fled from his face. "These poor, misguided people. They swear that they have renounced all the works of the Devil, and have come wholly into the arms of Mother Church. Yet again and again we find evidence that they are continuing their diabolical practices."

"Señor Padre."

Fray Antonio and Domingo both looked in surprise at Gaspar, who seldom spoke until he was spoken to, and often not then.

"Yes, my son?"

"Señor Padre, those thing—" Gaspar motioned back with his head in the general direction of the hacienda. "Those not Tano. Those thing Dinneh."

The padre's face lightened with relief. After all, the Franciscan missionaries had reached few of the roving Navajos. They were still children of nature, and less blameworthy than those Indians who had been instructed.

"But, Señor Padre."

"Yes, my son?"

"Here, in the plaza of the New Town, there is something—" Gaspar hesitated—

"Yes, my son?"

"Here is still one—what you call estufa—"

The priest's eyebrows shot upward. "You mean there remains one of the evil heathen shrines, here in the Villa? In this plaza, which has been cleansed and blessed? Where?"

Without more words, Gaspar led the way to a careless appearing heap of leaves and brush in the shadow of the chapel. While the padre and Domingo watched incredulously, he shoved aside the brush and poked out his lips toward an opening that led downward into darkness. Domingo had seen its like before. In the Santa Fe plaza the returning Spanish had found one of these underground worship chambers of the Pueblo Indians, called kiva in some of the Pueblos' language, and estufa, or stove, by the Spanish, perhaps because of their steamy heat. Different priests, Domingo thought, viewed the matter differently. One Santa Fe padre had lugged out the sinister paraphernalia and then had consecrated the place and celebrated Mass in it, the

Villa lacking adequate chapels. Other priests had thundered denunciations of the practice.

Fray Antonio said hopefully, "Surely this has not been used since the apostates repented and returned to Holy Church."

In answer, Gaspar indicated a sharply outlined footprint in the dust where the ladder led downward. Eloquently also he sniffed at the opening. The pit was redolent of Indian tobacco.

Fray Antonio's face darkened. Crossing himself, he girded his robe higher and thrust a cautious foot down upon the first ladder rung, the next and the next, testing their trustworthiness as he went. Profound silence in the depths of the kiva. Out of that silence the padre reappeared, his face set in stern lines, a buckskin-wrapped bundle reverently carried in one hand.

He spoke heavily. "A statue of Our Lady, and used in their unholy rites. I will reconsecrate her and return her to her place in the chapel. And I will fetch a brand from the fire and burn this outpost of hell." His voice quivered with wrath. "And they shall do penance for the sacrilege. Yea, they shall do heavy penance. We must root out the evil, even at the cost of lives."

For a moment he stared down at the statue, protruding from the folds of leather. Then he strode off toward the convent, his wrathful disappointment evidently blotting out all thought of the boys, who had stared at the Lady as intently as he. Had not these people partaken of the Sacrament, his solemnly shaken head seemed to be asking, even while they carried on their abominable worship of pagan gods?

With a jerk of the lips toward his retreating form, Gaspar said, "The statue. Like the Señorita your sister."

"Qué absurdo!" Domingo rapped out a flat denial. Then he admitted unwillingly, "It resembles the Conquistadors. That I saw for myself. The same wood carver may have fashioned both. And it has always been said that my mother looks like the Conquistador. And certainly my sister resembles our mother. That is all there is to it."

"The statue is like the Señorita Lucia," Gaspar repeated with unshaken conviction. "The same hair. The same very-very blue eyes."

"Qué absurdo," Domingo reiterated. But he spoke absently, glancing uneasily around the plaza.

Only one Tano was in sight. He was a tall Indian, with an unforgettable face. His nose was like an eagle's beak and his mouth a thin gash, while his coppery skin was deeply marked by past smallpox. With arms folded across his breast, he stood gazing away from the newly discovered kiva.

"That one called the Eagle," Gaspar said, his own lips motionless. "He saw."

Hastily the two boys mounted their waiting horses and trotted them home.

"Too soft!" Domingo was thinking as he relived the past hour. "Such is the padre whom Uncle Melchior thought too soft."

Chapter 6

New Ideas for Domingo

DOMINGO did not at once revisit New Town. Eager though he was to know what had happened after Fray Antonio strode away from the kiva, fear overcame curiosity. He was afraid of the padre's flaming wrath; afraid, too, of Fray Antonio's queer ideas. That anyone should question the right of a slaveholder to set his brand upon the flesh that he had purchased!

There was plenty of work to keep Domingo at home. As soon as Roque and Fernando had safeguarded the casa, by mending walls and making new gates, they had had to look after the fields. Though a part of the Rivera land had already been planted in corn, squash and beans by the Tanos,

64

the remainder must be tilled and planted without more loss of time. The men set to work with their iron-shod wooden plows in the sweet flat land that stretched eastward from the houses to the edge of the arroyo.

Old Rosa, heavy and short of breath though she was, could do a man's work around the house; but to make the place livable more than one man would be needed. The casa was a miniature walled village. To the west, toward the New Town, lay the family courtyard, with its south gates through which carretas could be driven, and, in one leaf of the gate, a door for foot passengers. This patio had rooms built around three sides, the sala, or living room, the dining room, the bedrooms, the priest's room. Between bedroom and sala on the west, a little arched passage, the zaguán, led into a high-walled garden.

The east side of the double courtyard belonged to the servants. A double row of rooms ran through the center, dividing the two portions from one another, and from the dining room in the master's court another zaguán led to the kitchen in the servants'. The service patio also was lined with rooms, each with a separate door opening on the court. For safety in Indian attack, all the rooms except the double row in the center were backed by outer walls unbroken save by a few small, high windows. Servants' rooms and kitchens filled the north and west sides, and against the east wall were the old storeroom or despensa, the old loom room, the smithy, and the carpenter shop. In the patio stood hornos, ovens shaped like old-fashioned beehives, where Rosa and her daughters did the baking.

Gaspar helped with the heavier work of restoring masters' bedrooms and sala, servants' quarters and kitchen. The re-building of dining room and priest's room must be postponed to a more leisured time. Smithy, loom room and carpenter shop were likewise out of repair, and must be put in usable shape as soon as possible, and there were the hard clay floors of the patios to be patched and smoothed again, and the little walled garden to be trimmed, pruned, replanted.

Tio Melchior escaped the domestic confusion and inconvenience of the restoration. He was a member of the first military scouting detail to make a circuit of the New Town territory, on the lookout for hostile Indians. Domingo, too, avoided most of the humdrum work. While the settlers had been issued a ration of corn for seed and food, it was by no means enough, and meat was badly needed to supplement it. It fell to Domingo to do the hunting for the Rivera estancia, with Gaspar accompanying him, since a lone hunter would have invited Indian attack.

Lucia grumbled about these hunting trips. "It is always the same," she fumed. "The boys and men have the fun and the excitement, and the girls never the least bit of it."

All morning she had worked with Lupe at whitewashing the sala wall. And when her mother had bidden her stop and rest a bit, she had also handed her another pair of Domingo's long stockings to mend while she rested. Lucia was perched on the well curb, impatiently thrusting her needle in and out, and watching her brother and Gaspar make ready to dash away on their horses.

"You would not like it so well as you seem to think, muchacha," Domingo informed her patronizingly. "You might be well pleased to take your ease at home if once you had to fight your way through miles of rough country, all cactus and thornbushes, to scare up a turkey or two. I think you would not like fetching in the game half so well as you like to eat it."

"Just give me a chance," muttered Lucia. "You would

find me perfectly willing to do my share of the hunting, I assure you."

Tia Nina, seated on the opposite side of the well, was embroidering a colcha, punctuating her work on the coverlet with many sighing pauses. At Lucia's declaration she shrieked softly. "How you can be so bold and unwomanly!" she reproached her. "I am sure I should faint dead away if I had to kill one of the sweet little rabbits your brother fetches home. And I should die of fear if I went out where Utes and Apaches might be hiding behind every tree. And, besides, the good Lord made women women and men men, and that is all there is to be said about it."

"It is a mystery to me why He had to plan it the way He did," Lucia grumbled. "I am sure if I had been He—"

"Hush, girl!" Tia Nina cried, crossing herself.

Doña Leonor did not scold, but she shook her head reprovingly, even while she softened the reproach by saying, "Daughter, I once felt the same way about it."

Tia Nina changed the subject. "Nephew, Old Rosa says the Santa Cruz store has copper thimbles from Mexico. Mine is jammed so that it will not stay on my finger. Will you get me a new one, please, tomorrow?"

So on the morrow Domingo went to New Town for the thimble, and saw Fray Antonio again. He was as gentle and kind as ever, and made no reference to the abominable kiva. The two boys stole curious glances in its direction: the concealing brush was gone, and a new cross surmounted a mound of fresh earth like a grave. Although no word was spoken, some of the Tanos who worked around the convento scowled more blackly than before, as if they might have felt the whip across their shoulders. The Eagle, Domingo noticed, was one of the most sullen.

That day Fray Antonio showed the boys the convent loom room, where Tanos, both men and women, were weaving wool from the mission sheep. The Pueblos, he said, had probably been weavers since back toward the world's dawn, making cotton cloth before the Spanish brought in wool. They had several types of loom, some of them not much inferior to the Mexican, which had probably been brought from Africa when the Spanish were fighting the Moors.

"The Dinneh weave," said Gaspar. "My mother weave."

Domingo thought surprisedly that he had never before heard Gaspar mention his mother.

"Does she weave mostly the strips of rabbitskin?" Fray Antonio inquired interestedly. "And maybe sandals of yucca fiber and the like? Of these I have seen admirable specimens."

Gaspar nodded assent.

"I have seen also looms which the Apache De Navahu copied from those of the Pueblos," the priest continued; "and these Navajo were weaving with woolen yarn."

Gaspar was studying the nearest weaver. On the great wooden loom the warp threads lay horizontal, and were lifted and dropped by the weaver's feet on two plank pedals. Wound on a bobbin that resembled a little dugout canoe, the yarn was carried through between the raised and lowered threads. The wool was of varied colors: ordinary white, brownish black, and gray made by carding and spinning white and black together. In addition to these natural hues there were yellow, dyed with rabbit brush, and yellowish green, from oak. The Tano was weaving stripes of yellow and gray, each edged with black.

"I think I can do this," said Gaspar.

Both Domingo and Fray Antonio scrutinized the Navajo's intent face. Domingo had always vaguely liked its appear-

ance, but until this moment he had never given it any conscious thought. The marred brow was low and broad, and
across it the eyebrows drew a strong black line. Below that
charcoal stroke, the eyes looked out straight and clear between thick, straight lashes. The nose was straight, and the
planes of the cheeks were flat. The only decided curve was
the curl of the upper lip, seen in profile. Straight, keen, intent, was Gaspar's face.

Fray Antonio rested one sandaled foot on a pedal of an
unused loom beside him, and his chin on his palm. He continued to gaze at Gaspar as he spoke musingly. "It would be
good to have you learn the weaving. But why not also the
reading and writing? The numbers?"

Blank silence answered him.

"Our traders," he went on, his eyes moving to Domingo's
face, "take advantage of the unlettered. You know how it is
about our money. We do not see coin from year's end to
year's end. Most business is done by barter, but there are
also several kinds of peso, all on paper or by word of mouth.
That, my lads, is where the trickery comes in. The silver
dollar—peso de plata—is worth eight reales; the peso de
proyecto six; the peso de antiguo, the old dollar, four. But
the dollar of the land, peso de la tierra, has a value of only
two." His face crinkled with laughing disgust, "If only God's
children would devote as much time and thought to the
problem of making an honest living as they do to schemes
for cheating their brothers!"

"But how do they use these pesos to cheat them, Father?"
Domingo asked respectfully.

"Simple, my boy. Let us say that they buy from a Tano
a blanket, and pay him one peso. That peso will be a dollar
of the land, worth two reales. They sell the blanket to an
Apache for two dollars, and you may be sure they are

dollars of silver, so the merchant gets sixteen reales worth in barter, a profit of fourteen reales. Dollars are dollars to an Indian, and could they be otherwise? To him money is a new conception. One of my countrymen bought a Mexican macaw for eight dollars. Its blue and yellow feathers he sold to the Indians for use in their diabolical rites—" the padre made the sign of the cross—"and for what amount do you suppose? For four hundred sixty-two dollars."

"So you think—?" Domingo questioned doubtfully.

"So I think it is needful to instruct our Spanish boys and as many of the Indians as we can persuade, not only in reading and writing, but in numbers as well. It will be slow work to gather in the Tano children again," he added regretfully. "Thus far I have only a few, whose parents are working in New Town, like Marco, the herder, and him they call the Eagle."

Domingo spoke hotly. "The Tanos are ungrateful and rebellious!"

Fray Antonio eyed him thoughtfully. "Remember that they have been forced out of their good houses, which they had built here for themselves. And though they begged our Governor General for time to harvest the crops they had put in, so that they might have food for the coming year, it seemed that this delay was impossible. Perhaps it was impossible. Yet the loss of their seed and their labor will be one more grievance to add to the bitterness in these primitive hearts. I pray that the gall may not overflow upon us as it did in the Great Revolt."

Domingo made a gesture of incredulous indignation.

"Do not forget that they held this land," the priest responded; "held all of it, and had built their solid villages and lived in them with no interference save from Apache,

Ute, Comanche. For who knows how many generations, how many centuries? Poor children, they thought this country was their own." The padre's face darkened, and he beat one palm with a clenched fist. "My lads, remember, and remember well, that nothing but the need to save their lost souls could give us the right to take their lands and their liberties. And whosoever uses violence for the sake of his own gain, I say to you that it were better for him that a millstone were hung about his neck and that he were drowned in the depths of the sea."

Domingo flinched from this thunder of denunciation, and thought again how fantastically his Uncle Melchior had erred in his estimate of this man.

As if he noticed Domingo's awe, Fray Antonio's face softened. "That curse would not fall on you, I am sure, my son," he said, regarding him keenly. "Greed is probably no sin of yours. But you will do a good deed and acquire merit if you see to it that Gaspar is given a chance to learn."

"He is not my slave," Domingo interposed stiffly. "He belongs to my uncle."

Fray Antonio's face crinkled with laughter again. Domingo had never seen a man's countenance that could show so many and varied emotions, like a clear pool that reflects the sky and all passing things. It was as if there were beneath it nothing that the padre need hide. "If you were to speak to the Señor Rivera—Doña Nina—" he suggested. "It is easily seen that her nephew is the apple of her eye. Another thing: you yourself might enjoy continuing with me your studies of rhetoric and law and theology. It would give me great pleasure to companion with a young gentleman who has had the advantage of university teaching in Mexico City."

So it was that when the boys went their way back to the hacienda, Domingo was feeling more comfortable. It was good to have the padre recognize him as a scholar and a gentleman. It would be good to return to his studies, which he liked better than Tio Melchior thought suitable. Only Tia Nina's intercession had enabled the boy to have his years at the university. Domingo had relished the few hours each day in the dim halls, with the learned padres who taught him a little theology, law and rhetoric, along with the use of the globes, and stories of the splendor of the Spanish conquests. In the sixteenth—and now in the seventeenth century —the great winged ships of Spain and Portugal had swept the seven seas. And wherever, in Peru, in the Indies, in the Philippines, in Mexico, the armed warriors had seized the land, there the padres had planted the cross.

As he considered his companion, however, Domingo's complacence wore thin. Why should the padre think Domingo responsible for Gaspar's education? And, in any case, if you sent all your slaves and servants to school, who would be left to do the everyday labor? And would not wholesale education turn the world upside down? Would men be satisfied to be slaves or even peones, if they knew as much as their masters? Would it not be unkind to make them discontented with their lot?

Domingo did not once look at Gaspar during the short canter to the hacienda, but his thoughts were with him if his eyes were not. Those thoughts leaped the two years to the time when Gaspar became a part of his daily life.

That was in Domingo's fourteenth year, when he had begged his uncle to take him along on the annual journey to Chihuahua, northwest of Mexico City. The yearly January Fair at Chihuahua was an assemblage of great importance and interest. Buyers and sellers came to it from all over Old Mexico, from all over New Mexico. Domingo would never forget the thrill and excitement of it: Indians of every tribe brought their wares, the Aztecs, Tlascalans and Tarahumaras from the south, the Pueblos and nomadic tribes from the north, who journeyed thither with fine pelts, and sometimes with captives to be sold as slaves. The Indians from the north bartered skins and turquoise and jet for parrot feathers and abalone shells, and sometimes they sold horses, which they must first have stolen, and bought burros and chickens. And always there was a lively trade in the sweet rich nuts of the piñon.

The Fair was a great, gaudy market, surging with strange people and strange merchandise, clattering with strange languages. Tio Melchior bought wrought-iron bridle ornaments and fancy trappings for Domingo's new saddle horse, Oro, and jewelry for Tia Nina and Doña Leonor and Lucia; mosaics which the Pueblos made from turquoise, shell and jet, set in pitch on shaped pieces of bone.

Then, as they were passing a part of the market where Indian captives were chained together awaiting buyers, Domingo noticed a boy who looked to be about his own age. Today, as he cantered with Gaspar along the road to the hacienda, he recalled with astonishment how small both he and Gaspar had been, only two years ago. In their fourteenth year or thereabouts, they had not begun to shoot up, much less to broaden out. Even then Domingo felt a jolting sickness at sight of the slim child, chained between a Ute woman and a Comanche warrior with shaved head and fierce forelock. The Indian boy's tangle of black hair stood out wildly, and he wore nothing but rags of buckskin and one plaited fiber sandal. The unshod foot was swollen and

bleeding from the long trek. Whenever the boy found anyone looking at him, he straightened his thin little shoulders
defiantly and scowled.

Domingo had tugged Tio Melchior's sleeve and pointed
at the boy. "Buy him, Uncle," he begged.

At first Uncle Melchior paid no attention. He shook
off his nephew's hand and went on talking to his friends.
Domingo did not give up. He kept tugging at the sleeve
and looking back at the Indian boy, until at last Tio Melchior stopped and listened, though impatiently, to what he
was saying.

The upshot was that he stared over his shoulder at the
captive, and then grumblingly returned and examined him,
feeling his flesh and peering at his teeth and eyes. Seeing
that the boy was a sound specimen, in spite of his scrawniness,
Uncle Melchior dickered with his owner and made the
purchase.

The whole incident had flitted through Domingo's mind
before he and Gaspar had reached the hacienda, dismounted
and gone their ways, Gaspar to the east courtyard, Domingo
to the west.

Finding Lucia working with their mother at the muslin
wall covering, while Tia Nina sat near them, pretending
to embroider, Domingo dropped on one of the colchones
and watched them.

He did not speak until Lucia's work brought her to his
side. "Gaspar would never wish to study reading and writing and numbers, do you think?" he murmured.

Holding the muslin shoulder high against the wall, his
sister looked down at him in bright-eyed amazement. "What
made you think of such a thing?" she inquired.

He told her of the conversation with Fray Antonio. "But

I think, myself," he concluded, "that education would only make him unhappy, since he is a slave."

He had kept his voice low, but Tia Nina always listened when her nephew spoke. "She seizes Domingo's words as if each were a pearl," Lucia often grumbled. Now the aunt dropped her work on the steep slope of her lap, down which it promptly coasted to the floor.

"Your uncle will say that the padre is a dreamer," she warned them, wheezily. "Don Melchior will be angry if you try to take the boy from his work and turn his head with clerkly learning. It is not God's will that the lower orders should be educated above themselves. And I should like to know why Gaspar should read and write when neither your mother nor I can do so."

And I doubt if Tia Melchior knows much more than to sign his name, Domingo was thinking, *which, to be sure, is more than most of the settlers can do*. The muster roll had been largely signed with crosses in place of names.

"Above themselves, Tia Nina?" Lucia protested, her funny little nose twitching. "But why would it be above Gaspar? Domingo says that the boy is as smart as Don Coyote himself."

To all this Doña Leonor said nothing. Tia Nina talked so much that her younger sister-in-law had cultivated a habit of stillness. In spite of her silence, her large eyes were widening and narrowing so thoughtfully that Domingo wondered uneasily what was in her mind.

"Old Juan will need Gaspar with the lambing," Tia Nina continued to fret. "May is a busy month for people of the land. You know that very well, Lucia."

"Tia mia," her niece said coaxingly, "Old Juan is forever bragging that he could manage this small flock alone and with one hand tied behind him. When our sheep have multiplied, it will be a different matter."

The discussion had not eased Domingo's mind, and presently he excused himself and went out where he might find quiet to think. Lucia followed him, her face alive with eagerness.

"Querido," she said, though she was seldom so soft as to call her brother "beloved," "I know exactly how you feel. You are so much kinder than most men; you are somewhat like our father, Madre says. What are you planning to do about it? Help with Gaspar's chores, I suppose, so that he may have a little time to study with Fray Antonio? Oh, brother, you are really wonderful!"

"You take entirely too much for granted!" Domingo snapped.

There she was doing it again, he thought as he strode away from her. She was taking his mere questioning thoughts as solid facts to be acted upon without loss of time. Lucia often made her brother both cross and uncomfortable.

Chapter 7

Witchcraft!

DURING the next weeks nothing more was said about Gaspar's education. Talk would have served no purpose, for the Navajo boy's time was fully occupied in the work of the estancia. In the first place, Old Juan did need his help with the lambing. Roque and Fernando had all they could possibly do in plowing and planting and in woodwork and leathercraft for the new church that was to be built in Santa Cruz as well as for the Rivera casa.

The lambs were few, to be sure, but both they and their mothers needed more than the normal amount of attention. That was because of the insufficient forage. The spring and early summer were so dry that Uncle Melchior's pasture land had scanty growth, and the ewes were weak and thin in consequence. The scarcity of good browse had driven some to eat chokecherry and whorled milkweed and loco. Some had cropped so close in their hunger that they had worn down their mouths and had consumed more earth than was good for them.

"The poor, poor things!" Lucia moaned, when she and her mother went out to inspect them.

Sheep always looked mournful, partly because of the glands in the corners of their eyelids, which resembled great, unshed tears. Only the lambs ever showed any spring and gaiety, and this May even they lacked it, being too ill-nourished. Their mothers were reluctant to feed them, and Old Juan and Gaspar had to straddle the poor ewes and hold them fast until their infants had had a chance to nurse.

"Only Silver seems as bold and joyous as ever," Lucia observed. "And what a big boy he is getting to be!"

Silver was playing his favorite game, challenging his comrades from a little hillock and butting them off the minute they took his dare.

"That one!" Old Juan looked up from the tiny soft lamb he was attending. "He is strong enough to get his share and half the next one's. And he is smart enough to find green stuff if there is green stuff to find. Señorita," he went on, "would you care to try your hand at cosseting this little ewe lamb and yonder little buck as well? The mother of the buck has died, and the other had twins and will not allow this little ewe to come near her. She left her to die, unlicked and starving."

Nodding her agreement, Lucia eagerly gathered up her skirt, and let Old Juan lay the frail infants in it. As she and her mother returned to the house, they met Fray Antonio

approaching the gate. "Pobre pobrecitos!" she was croon-
ing. "Poor, poor little ones! Oh, Señor Padre!" she interrupted herself at sight of the priest.

"Buenas tardes, Señora y Señorita!" the padre greeted
them, lifting his hand in blessing. "Señorita, would you like
to add to your nursery? The mission flock also has its orphans. Marco is doing well—fairly well—but it is only the
women who have the patience required for these criaturas. If
you wish to adopt them, my daughter, they are yours."

Lucia curtsied, lambs and all, her many petticoats swish-
ing gaily. "Oh, padre, muchas gracias!" she thanked him.
"I shall be building a flock of my very own."

"Thank you indeed, padre," Doña Leonor said. "Lucia
will gladly accept the trust. And now it is near dinnertime.
Will you honor us by eating at our table?"

"Already you have made it homelike here," the padre
commented, as they entered the shady portal.

Lucia hastened to put her foundlings in a sunny corner,
where they huddled together like kittens. Old Juan said
that sunshine was medicine to the weakly lambs.

When Lucia rejoined her mother and the padre, Fray
Antonio was seating himself in the one chair, to which Doña
Leonor had motioned him.

"A woman's touch!" he was saying, as he approvingly
surveyed the room.

The sala had indeed changed in the weeks since the
Riveras' arrival. Rosa, Lupe and Gaspar, with Domingo
occasionally helping, had mended the clay roof and the ceiling. It was a beautiful ceiling, short lengths of willow sticks,
painted red and blue and fitted together in herringbone
pattern. Soledad was not able to climb about just now, for
she had a new baby, a tiny girl, as soft and fragile as Lucia's
lambs.. Lucia took Soledad's place, helping whitewash the

walls with powdered gypsum that the Indians had traded
them for a pair of Castilian chickens. And she and her
mother had stretched the muslin around the lower part of
the wall, to keep the whitewash from rubbing off on the
backs and shoulders of those who sat on the colchones.

Above the muslin wainscot hung two or three treasured
mirrors in gilt frames, and others in wrought tin; and there
were painted pictures of the saints, and a shrine for the
Virgin Mary, while the Santo Niño which Doña Leonor especially loved sat serenely on his silver chair in a niche over
the fireplace. All these had traveled up from Mexico City in
the Riveras' big wooden and leather chests.

The smooth clay floor was partially covered by strips
of hand-woven wool carpeting, white striped with black.
Against the wall were low divans, which were merely the
wool-stuffed mattresses or colchones, doubled over and
covered with bright serapes. At night they were unfolded
and became beds.

Fernando had already made one table, with the corners
decoratively carved, and Roque had tanned and painted a
leather cover for it. Fernando had also fashioned the elbow
chair in which the padre was sitting, as well as several stools.
Altogether, it had begun to feel like home, and would be
still more so when more color was added. Lucia had the
promise of a warm pink wash for the front house walls,
behind the portales. She had decided that the rosy color,
contrasting with the neutral adobe and the deep soft blue of
the window frames and doors, would lend more gaiety than
the blue she had first asked for. Color would add to the
charm of the whole patio, Lucia thought, pausing a moment
in the zaguán, and looking back into the sunny court, before
going to the kitchen. There, as her mother had bidden her,

she told Rosa and her daughters that the padre was to be
their guest at dinner.

Rosa looked out at the sun, and moaned. "Too late to
kill a chicken! The reverend Father will have to do with
these rabbits. To be sure, they are nice rabbits."

"They smell heavenly enough to please a padre," Lucia
assured her, dipping a ladle into the copper kettle which
simmered on Rosa's estufa. "Hot, hot, hot!" she squealed,
jumping up and down and sticking out her tongue to cool it.

"Not too much chili, please God?" Rosa asked in alarm,
jumping up herself, to peer questioningly into Lucia's swimming eyes.

Lucia shook her head vigorously. "Hot—from fire," she
mumbled between parted lips.

"In that case it serves you very right," Rosa declared
severely. "You act like a child, not like a young lady."

Convulsively Lucia swallowed the morsel, and said "ah-
wah-wah," tapping her open mouth to cool it. Then she
twitched Rosa's gray-streaked black braid and dipped from
the kettle another bit, which she blew on gustily. "It is very-
very good, Rosa," she said, when she had popped it into her
mouth. "Never can I grow so sedate that I shall act lady-
like about your cooking."

Rosa's face twitched into a gratified smile. "More speed
with those tortillas," she ordered her daughter Lupe, to
hide her pleasure in the señorita's flattery.

Lupe was kneeling at her task, resonantly slapping the
blue corn cakes thinner and thinner between her strong brown
palms. Obediently she stepped up her tempo, pausing only
to flop over on the griddle those that were half-baked, and
to replace finished ones with raw.

Lucia liked kitchens. Already, though Rosa had reigned

over this one only a few weeks, it was a homy and appetiz-
ing place, with braids of onions and garlic hanging from the
vigas, interspersed with ristras of dark red chili peppers,
which Rosa had fetched along. In addition, there were
bundles of new herbs which she gathered on the rancho and
hung from the ceiling poles to dry; verbena and wild onion,
mint and tansy mustard. Corn was stacked at one side, near
the stone metates where it would be ground, and cornhusks,
clean and white, were piled ready for all manner of uses,
for wrapping tamales and fritos before cooking, and for
cigarettes.

While the baking and some other cooking were done in the
hive-shaped ovens in the courtyard, Rosa had other stoves.
Chief among them was her estufa, built like a waist-high
box of adobe bricks, and with holes in the top where kettles
and pots could stand, each over its individual fire. She
used also the big corner fireplace, where something was always simmering in kettles or in earthenware pots that stood
on long-handled iron stands, so that they could easily be
pulled out on the hearth.

The air was richly flavored by the slow-cooking rabbits,
with their seasonings of marjoram and cummin and sage
and chili, and by frying beans, and by green chili, which
made a sauce that was scorching hot but delicious. Lucia
took a fresh tortilla and dipped out on it a little of the green
chili. She folded the tortilla over the sauce and nibbled
delicately, avoiding Rosa's irritated glance. The New Mexico climate made Lucia ravenous, and since there was a guest
and only one chair and four stools, she knew she was likely
to have to await her dinner until after the rest had eaten.

"If you would please to set the table, Señorita," Old
Rosa suggested with a severe lift of the brows. "Soledad's
baby is ailing, and she is too busy with the criatura to help."

"M-m-m-m-m," Lucia murmured sorrowfully, her mouth full of food. "I hope the little thing will soon be better, Rosa."

"If not, heaven will have one angel more." Old Rosa's tone was sad but submissive. The death of the babies was one of the bitter facts of this frontier life.

"Little love!" Lucia murmured again, and almost choked on the tortilla because of the crowding tears.

Running through the zaguán once more, she got one of the best linen cloths from her mother's chest and the treasured silver from Tia Nina's. Lucia's parents had lost their silver at the time of the Revolt. As soon as she had arranged the table and placed the dishes, Lucia sought the kitchen again, and while Rosa was carrying a great pottery dish of rabbit into the sala, Lucia hurriedly rummaged in the kettle and fished out a fine hind leg for herself. She wrapped it in another tortilla, exchanging friendly glances with Lupe, who also was nibbling, and beat a retreat to a far corner of the service patio, where she could enjoy the prize in peace.

After dinner came the siesta. The men rested in the sala, Tia Nina asking the padre's pardon because the priest's room next to the entrance had not yet been rehabilitated. Doña Leonor, Doña Nina and Lucia withdrew to the colchones in the bedrooms.

Even outdoors it was quiet. The cicadas sang a high, sleepy song in the cottonwoods, an occasional hen cackled, an occasional rooster crowed. These sounds came drowsily through open doors, and the only other noises were the buzz of flies and Tia Nina's prodigious snoring. Even Lucia did not mind the siesta. It was as invariable a part of the day's pattern as going to bed at night and eating the four meals: el desayuno, el almuerzo, la comida and la cena, with an extra one thrown in when food was not so scarce.

Siesta over, Roque yoked the oxen, and the padre and the womenfolk climbed into the carreta and went jogging the quarter-mile to town. Domingo and Gaspar had mounted their horses, waiting half-asleep in the patio, and trotted on ahead.

The women were bound for the small store. Rosa wanted some kitchen supplies, and Tia Nina hoped to find candied anise, of which she was fond, since wagons were said to have come up from Mexico City and Michoacan Province.

They had hardly turned in at the entrance to Santa Cruz when they saw that excitement was afoot. A small crowd had knotted before the chapel, and more people were running to join it, the children wriggling between grown-up legs to see better. Fray Antonio strode toward the noisy throng, the others following. Only the Señoras Rivera remained in the carreta, where they could see a little and at the same time preserve their dignity. Lucia scurried away before her mother or aunt could call her back. Old Rosa waddled along behind her, puffing breathlessly, and Domingo and Gaspar had tied their horses and were already in the thick of things. Lucia pushed toward them.

The center round which the throng had gathered was an Indian woman. She was not one of the Pueblos, Lucia thought. Her hair and dress differed from theirs, and she was slim and straight as a mature Pueblo woman seldom was. Though her weathered face showed her to be in the thirties, she had the lithe erectness of a girl. It was difficult to tell whether she was frightened or angry, for her head was proudly upflung, and her face masklike in its stillness. She stood unmoving, while the settlers threatened her with words and fists, and called, "El alcalde!" insistently, until they caught sight of Fray Antonio. Then the murmur, "Nuestro padre!" replaced the angry shout for the mayor, and the crowd parted to let "our padre" through.

Swinging round in front of the woman as if to shield her, Fray Antonio lifted his hand for silence. "Now what is all this unseemly clamor, my children?" he asked. "Daughter, what have you done that they assail you?"

Quieting with a gesture the medley of voices that responded to the question, he fixed kind eyes on the accused.

The woman spoke quietly in Spanish. "Padre, I do nothing."

Cries followed her words. "Witchcraft!" "A bruja!" "A witch of the Apaches de Navahu!" "The evil eye!" And from two women who had all along brandished the most vehement fists rolled a flood of malediction.

"Silence!" Fray Antonio commanded. "Doña Ana, let me hear your story."

"This Indian woman, she is a witch," Doña Ana declared. "Without a shadow of a doubt, padre. Out of nowhere she appears and into nowhere she vanishes."

"She is a daughter of the church," Fray Antonio defended her. "During my weeks in New Town she has been faithful at Mass. Her children have been baptized into Holy Church. Your accusation of witchcraft is a grave one, Doña Ana."

"If she is a daughter of the church, then why does she wear the Indian charms?" someone called from the crowd. "Look! Look at the white shell like a kernel of corn, tied into the knot of her hair."

The padre did not turn, but everyone else craned to see. After a glance at the amulet in the woman's chignon, Lucia continued to contemplate her face. It held an unexplained interest for her, like something that had been a part of her life as the mocking bird's song had been, or the fragrance of camellias—or of tortillas. Perhaps that look of pleasant familiarity lay merely in the woman's tribal resemblance to Gaspar.

"What has she done, that you accuse her?" Fray Antonio asked the people.

Doña Ana breathed so gustily that her words refused to come out, and her son Salvador elbowed forward and answered for her, with a sidelong glance at Lucia even in his self-important excitement. "What has she done?" he cried, in a voice that passed suddenly from a deep rumble to a high squeak. "She has brought my poor mother to death's door, that is what she has done."

Doña Matilde, the other of the two most vociferous women, shrilled out, "Me as well as Doña Ana! Me she touched at the altar two weeks ago. On my back, at the point nearest my heart—" Doña Matilde dramatically clutched her shoulder—"likewise Doña Ana, who was on her other side. And touching us, she muttered a curse. And we felt our hearts beat sharply, and our flesh crawl. And from that day we dwindle. Our bones ache. Our hair falls." She wrenched at her hair and glared around her.

"Daughter, what answer do you make?" Fray Antonio inquired without turning his head.

Again the Navajo spoke with dignity, in halting Spanish. "I say no curse. I say only a few words for 'Excuse me,' as I would say it in Dinneh, since I forget how it goes in Spanish. I say, in Dinneh, I do not mean to push against them."

"Lies, lies!" snarled Doña Ana, by this time enough recovered to talk. "She should be thrown in chains into the jail, padre, and a trial held."

Fray Antonio was silent a moment, as if in thought. Then he spoke suddenly, pointing to the far side of the plaza.

"Is not that the alcalde, there yonder?"

Doña Ana and Doña Matilde whirled around to look. So did everyone else, except Lucia and Gaspar. Lucia had been studying those two faces, Gaspar's and the woman's, and so she happened to witness a puzzling interchange. Just as she thought the padre murmured, "Right of asylum, daughter! Take church, and quickly!" she saw Gaspar's lips shoot out in their usual Indian gesture toward the half-open chapel doors. Gaspar's hand went to his breast as if saying, "I!" Gaspar's eyes lifted to the sun and dropped to the place of its setting. The sentence he thus spoke was quicker than speech, and clearer to the Indian woman than the padre's words had been. With a silent, all-of-a-piece movement, she slipped through the opening into the chapel.

"Aye!" shrieked Doña Ana, turning back from her glance across the plaza. "Aye! the witch is vanished!"

The crowd murmured angrily.

"Let us go to our houses and meditate upon this thing," Fray Antonio said in a deep, deliberate voice, and closed the chapel door behind him.

Slowly the people dispersed, some reluctant, some afraid, the accusers and Salvador jerking rebellious heads and growling. Some gazed searchingly at the chapel, and others cast quick glances at the four corners of the plaza. But they went.

Seeking the store, the Riveras made a few purchases before they creaked home in the ox-drawn carreta behind Domingo's high-stepping Gold and Gaspar's shambling gray. Tia Nina chattered excitedly all the way, and Old Rosa made a bee-line for the kitchen as soon as she had helped Doña Nina descend from the carreta. Immediately Lucia could hear the outcries, the exclamations of wonder and fear, that greeted Rosa's story.

Tio Melchior was off on an extra scouting trip, because of the growing uneasiness among the Pueblo Indians, so the rest of the family could talk with greater freedom as they ate. Tia Nina went over and over the episode, her voice shaken with the fear of witchcraft that they all felt in varying degrees, and yet keen with relish for anything that broke the monotony of her isolated life.

Did they not all see the shell in the heathen woman's knot of black hair? she demanded. Doña Leonor said, No, she certainly did not. In fact, looking from the carreta, and with the crowd between, she could not even make out the woman's face, not with any clarity. Of course, Tia Nina admitted, she, with her poor eyes, could not make her out, either, but had not Domingo and Lucia seen the shell? They had! Well, then! And could anyone deny that Doña Ana and Doña Matilde had lost flesh until they were living skeletons?

Doña Nina took a deep breath and started off in another direction. What kind of excuse was that, she asked, for the Indian woman to offer—that she had only begged the pardon of her poor victims? Did she not speak fair enough Spanish when she wished? Why would she drop into that heathen gibberish unless it was to utter curses? And what kind of foolish talk was this, that she had taken church— taken refuge in the holy place? Was that not the last place a witch would choose? Truly, if you asked Tia Nina, it was far more likely that the Navajo had used her evil arts to vanish into thin air.

For a few minutes Doña Nina ate busily, frowning as if in concentrated thought. Then she began again. Did they not see the heathen shell in the woman's hair? Well, then! You could not argue down the thing your eyes saw, could you? And no one could deny that Doña Ana and Doña Matilde—

As usual, Doña Leonor spoke little, though she looked flushed and uneasy. As for Domingo, he continually tried to turn the talk to other matters. Did they know that Plata's horns were pushing out into view? Yes, in truth, four little knobs, plain as the nose on your face. And Old Juan said he was as smart a buck lamb as ever he saw, and might one day make a better flock leader than the old gray goat.

"But mark my words," put in Tia Nina, who had gazed abstractedly ahead of her as she ate, not heeding even the conversation of her favorite Domingo, "Mark my words, this is by no means the end of the trouble. Call Gaspar, Rosa, call Gaspar and let us ask him what the shell in her hair would indicate."

Old Rosa willingly waddled off, but soon returned, shrugging and making eloquent gestures with hands, elbows, eyebrows and lips, all at once. "No Gaspar!" she announced. "He is gone. Also his horse."

Tia Nina shrieked her triumphant horror. "Did I not warn you? Evil things are afoot. And it is plain that you can trust no Navajo. The gray too! I always told Don Melchior that the boy should be content with a burro. And now what do you think of the white shell?"

It was only a little later that Gaspar appeared out of the deep twilight and said in a quiet voice, "Doña Nina, you send for me, no?"

Lucia shot a quick look at him, but he appeared quite as usual. Nor did he speak differently, save that he breathed a trifle fast.

"And where have you been?" Doña Nina demanded.

"The sheep—Old Juan—" Gaspar replied respectfully.

Tia Nina looked baffled, but she was evidently not done with Gaspar, and Lucia awaited her next words anxiously.

They did not come. Tia Nina's lips parted for them, but her mouth remained open and empty of speech, as her eyes rolled in alarmed question toward the patio entrance. From the direction of Santa Cruz sounded a small tumult. It rose in volume, the thud of hoofs mingled with the rush of feet and with shouting.

"Come along, Gaspar!" Domingo cried, with a meaning dart of the eyes.

The boys were gone before anyone could stop them. Nor did they go alone. Lucia had slipped out after them and attached herself firmly to her brother's coattails.

"Let me go! Let me go with you!" she begged.

She asked without real hope, as she so often did. This time, to her frightened delight, Domingo only grunted absent-minded disapproval and gave her a hand up. He was in the saddle and she was sitting behind him gripping him around the waist. They were out of the gate and on the road in the thick of the throng. Through the crowd they rode pell-mell, scattering the runners right and left.

Onward they pelted, to the east boundary of Uncle Melchior's rancho and the van of the little mob. But what was this? The van no longer advanced. The leaders were in full retreat.

It was a rout. Horses were swung round in a swift arc, reined back on their haunches, champing their bits and shaking the foam from their mouths in the moonlight. The people running behind them were leaping wildly aside to save themselves. Lucia clung to her brother and shut her eyes and wished that she had not been so bold.

"Look, Lucia! Look! The tower!" Domingo cried.

Fearfully she opened her eyes and peered ahead. When

she saw the tower on her mother's old hacienda, she did not wonder at the terror of the rabble.

"The witch! The witch! The Navajo witch!" they were shrieking in panic.

"Padre Nuestro, Qué estas en los cielos"—others were gabbling, since witches were notably powerless before the "Our Father."

Still others called futilely for somebody—anybody—named Juan to draw a circle round the tower. Everyone knew that men named Juan had authority over witches. If a Juan drew a circle round a witch, in whatever form she might have taken refuge, she could not move from the circle until he freed her.

Lucia herself was shaken by her own heartbeats as she looked at the tower. A pale figure stood in one of its windows—floated across it and presently stood at another, also visible from the road: a pale figure that exuded a bluish glow and glimmer.

Domingo and Gaspar were reining in their horses, swinging them around. Within two minutes they were galloping into the home patio, and Domingo was shouting for Roque or Fernando to come and bar the gate.

Chapter 8

And Exorcism

FOR DAYS the Navajo witch and her escape were the topic of every conversation in Santa Cruz and the surrounding haciendas. On that unholy night one of the settlers had gone to his housetop at dusk, and he swore that he saw a ghostly gray horse gallop away from the chapel door and out at the entrance of the villa, where the guards—who swore on their side that they had seen neither hide nor hair of such a steed—had seemed to make no effort to intercept it. The settler declared also that the fleeing mount carried two riders. But after the mob had taken up the chase and had been halted by the diabolical light in the tower, they had discounted the two riders. The witch had conjured up a horse, they concluded, and had used it to escape her due punishment.

Tio Melchior, returning from his scouting trip, listened gravely to the story. "Surely you remember," he said to the señoras, "what our Maria told us at the time of the Revolt? About Popé, the San Juan Indian who planned and led the rising?"

Doña Leonor nodded quick assent. Doña Nina, crossing herself and shuddering, implored her husband to go on.

"This Popé repaired to a certain cave, which no one else dared enter, and there he had concourse with powerful spirits, who told him what he was to do. And whenever he emerged from that place, he shone in the darkness, dimly and horribly, like a great glowworm."

"But Popé is dead," Tia Nina quavered.

"True. But witchcraft does not die. If one could possess that power, why not another? At any rate, we will all stay clear of the accursed tower. It is well that you have not secured the grant to the old hacienda, hermana mia," he congratulated his sister. "Who knows what misfortune it might have brought you? Even the soldier who made petition for it has no stomach for it now that this has happened. He says he will at once withdraw his suit."

"But the place is so near! So near!" Tia Nina whimpered, staring at him like a frightened baby, and dry-washing one pincushion hand with the other.

"Certainly Fray Antonio would exorcise the evil spirits," Doña Leonor suggested soothingly.

Next day Domingo went after the padre. He led a horse for him to ride, but Fray Antonio said he would rather walk the half-mile. Domingo demurred. Carrying the needed churchly objects, aspergillum and holy water and holy book? he asked. With his usual free stride impeded by the surplice and stole that the rite necessitated? Even so, Fray Antonio replied, smiling benignly.

So Domingo walked with him and led both mounts, until they reached the rancho, where the friar bade him good-by. To Lucia, Domingo recounted their conversation during the quarter-mile walk.

"Padre," he had burst out, when the two of them were alone on the road that led mournfully between half-dead orchards, "Padre, I assure you that the light resembled no rushlight or candle or torch that ever I saw. What could it have been, if not witchcraft?"

"Son, I do not know."

"You do not doubt that I saw it, father?"

"No, assuredly. I question only its supernatural origin."

Open-mouthed, Domingo stared at him. The first part of the adventure was reasonably clear and matter of fact in the boy's mind, since his sister had added her information to his own theories. Fray Antonio had reminded the Navajo woman of her legal right of asylum in the church, and when she showed no understanding of the words, Gaspar had reënforced them with signs that were intelligible to her. Then the padre, when she had slipped out of sight behind him, had closed the chapel door, leaving it unlocked so that Gaspar, returning at dusk, could carry her away.

So much, Domingo understood. But what about the spectrally glowing figure? Following so closely on his discovery of the unholy bundle of sticks at the foot of the same tower, the blue light made Domingo's flesh crawl, even in memory. Helplessly he asked, "What could it have been, save witchcraft?"

"Witchcraft," the padre echoed him, and crossed himself. "Who dare doubt the existence of evil powers? But this strange glow—bluish and sickly, you say? Domingo, my son, have you seen decaying wood flicker and gleam in the night? Was this apparition similar?"

Domingo's brows flew to a peak and he nodded hesitatingly.

"I have often wondered about Popé and his guiding spirits and the aura of awful light he sometimes carried," the padre mused. "Popé was a clever man, and mighty. Not often do leaders rise among our Indians, I do not know quite why. And the tribes seldom work together long enough to accomplish any one great purpose, good or ill. For a time they may sweep on in unison, as ocean breakers sweep mightily toward shore. But soon their force spends itself, and they fall apart, as separate as the drops of water. Even Popé, when he seemed to have accomplished his wicked end, waxed foolish in his pride. He tricked himself out in the finery of dead Spaniards, and draped himself in the vestments of the Church, and mimicked the ceremonies of those whom he had destroyed or driven away."

Domingo blinked respectfully, wondering what connection there could be between Popé and the Navajo witch.

"Popé knew that no ordinary leadership could hold together the different Pueblo tribes until they had done his dreadful work," Fray Antonio went on, gazing abstractedly at the puffs of dust cast up by his plodding sandals. "So he appealed to their superstitious fears. It is said that he could invoke the fire in the kiva and bring forth clouds like the cumulus clouds that the Pueblos so venerate. I myself know herbs that make dense white billows of smoke when cast upon the fire. I have wondered whether Popé may not have used such herbs; and whether he may not also have devised in some equally clever fashion the horrid shining of his body—"

Silently they trudged onward, Domingo revolving in his mind these startling new suggestions. At length Fray Antonio spoke again.

"It is a grievous thing to attach to another soul the stigma of witchcraft. Suppose this Navajo woman had been imprisoned? Who knows how long her trial might have endured? And even after the civil authorities were done, the masters of the Inquisition might have taken her in hand."

Domingo shuddered. The Inquisition had ended in Spain, but in Mexico and New Mexico it was still mighty. Witches, Domingo knew, were held in heavy iron chains and tested by torture.

"The right of asylum itself entails hardship," Fray Antonio said. "True, any man may shelter himself in the holy place so long as he will. True, he need answer no questions, not if the King himself were to ask them. Yet even so—"

Domingo smiled faintly. It had always seemed farcical to him that the questioner could put to the fugitive all manner of incriminating questions, and that the fugitive need only reply, parrotlike, "My name is church. My name is church."

"Even so," the padre continued, "what might be the end of it all for the Navajo woman? And, in the meantime, what of her innocent children?"

They had reached the casa gate of the Riveras. "From here," said Fray Antonio, "I go alone. I find the woman, God willing, and with his blessing learn whether or no she is a witch."

Hours passed before the padre returned, hours while the Rivera household fidgeted with fearful eagerness. But when at length Fray Antonio entered the patio, his serene face calmed them.

"All is well," he said. "I found our sister at last, and ascertained that she is no witch. Without faltering she repeated the whole of The Lord's Prayer."

Tia Nina sighed deeply. "A sure test. Though is it not surprising that a Navajo should know the words?"

"Gaspar can repeat it as fast as anyone," Domingo reminded her.

"And Maria," Doña Leonor added. "She also could."

"To the tower I have given the benediction of Holy Church," the padre continued.

"The bundle of heathen sticks—?" Domingo ventured.

The padre's face grew solemn. "Those I burned with fire, and for their use I imposed a penance. The woman repented. She had thought it safer to propitiate her heathen gods, in case they might still have power, although she says that she follows them no longer."

With a surge of daring, Domingo wished that he might have been there, to see the rites of exorcism and benediction. He could picture the padre, sprinkling holy water over the woman and around the tower, while he chanted the awful words of curse and blessing.

That day's events quieted the fears of the people. Nevertheless, they kept at a distance from the tower, and even from the old rancho, so as not to see the unholy lights if they should reappear. And the Navajo woman came no more to the chapel at Santa Cruz.

Chapter 9

G for Gaspar

MEANTIME, the threat of hunger grew more menacing, and diverted the settlers' minds from the threat of witchcraft. The dry springtime had ripened into a sere and dusty summer, and crops were poor, both in the fields the Tanos had planted, and in those the Spanish had tilled after their arrival. The additional seed corn, cattle and implements that had been promised the colonists did not come, and the people grumbled. Uncle Melchior ordered his household to put aside for next year's seed a good portion of their corn, and Tia Nina was beginning to fret at the meager meals that were their lot.

Old Juan was giving the flock more than his usual care,

since the possibility of famine made it doubly important.
Juan knew always where to look for the best forage, and
when there was nothing else, he would dig up certain roots
and split them with his ax, and the sheep would eat them
eagerly. When shearing time came and Lucia and her
mother went out to see the fun, they found the flock in fair
condition, despite their scanty pasture.

When Doña Leonor praised his skill, Old Juan responded
with respectful familiarity. "It is needful, as you know,
Señora, to see that the creatures eat regularly, one day like
another, even though the food be poor, and that they have
their fill of water no less than once every two days. When
they feast for a month and fast for a day, look you what
happens: their wool records the brief fasting with a weak
spot in its length. And there it breaks in carding, and does
not spin into so good a yarn."

Old Juan pulled a lock from a fleece newly shorn, and
showed them what he meant. "I admit that the whole fleece
weighs little better than a pound," he went on, "and that it
has so much of this hairy over coat that merino breeders
would declare it worthless. Yet when there is no break, no
weakening of the fiber through neglect, this wool cards like a
dream, smoothing out soft and fluffy. It lacks the heavy
covering of grease that some wools have, and the tight
crimp of the merino, which is hard to card out and which
leaves lumps and knots in the yarn when the women have
spun it."

Lucia listened wonderingly to Old Juan's stream of talk.
For the most part he spoke seldom, and then in short, sharp
phrases, lightened with flashes of dry humor. He was so
much alone, he said, that his tongue grew rusty, though he
did talk, and even sing, to the flock and Chepe. But bring
him in and let the ear of his mistress be turned toward him,

and he could talk interminably about the sheep, their wool and their browse.

"This is what you call the kemp?" Doña Leonor said inquiringly, touching certain shorter, thicker fibers that bristled from the wool. "And it is undesirable, Juan?"

He nodded profoundly. "Si, si, si, Señora. It is very bad. But little by little we shall breed it out."

"It is what sticks out of the serape and tickles when you sit on it," Lucia commented, peering at the wool.

Old Juan nodded again. Then, with a swoop, he seized Silver, who had been petted so much that he stayed around human beings more than did any other members of the flock. Parting his wool with a skilful hand, Juan showed them that it was thicker, whiter and more springy than the fleece he had been showing them. "You see: very little kemp here. This one will be a father and a father of fathers, passing on his superior wool to many-many lambs."

"It will take long—long," Doña Leonor mused, contemplating the pitifully small band. "Juan, you remember the splendid shearings of the old days, before the Revolt."

At the words, Old Juan looked more than ever like one of the mischief-loving duendes of Spanish legend, or the equally roguish dwarfs of some of the Pueblo tales, the choogy-ays. Within the frame of bristling hair and vast, outstanding ears, his face crinkled into leathery wrinkles of laughter.

"Si, Señora," he assented, chuckling. "How could I forget? The peones coming from all the ranchitos up and down the Canyon of the Neighbors, and from the Villa, and all falling to at the shearing. And the gentlefolk looking on, and visiting, and eating, and drinking. And you in the sala holding your bailes, and we in the courtyard as happy with our fandangos! We must set that Roque to work making new fiddles and guitars against the day."

944986

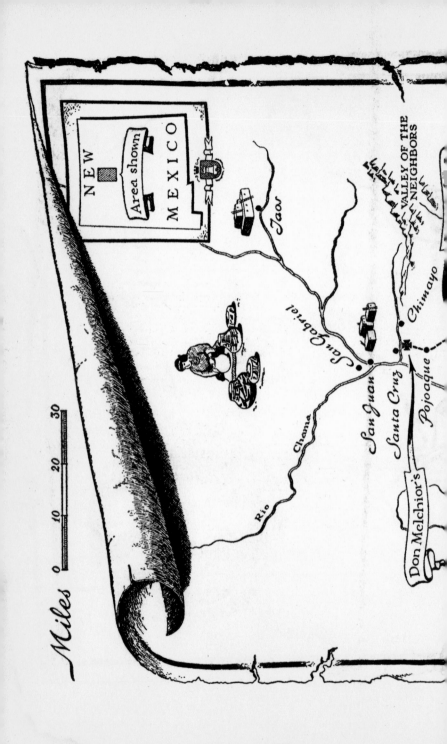

The Country
of
"The Silver Fleece"

Pecos

Pecos

Rio

Rio Grande

L.R.Tschirky

Lucia clapped her hands like a child. "We shall really have fiestas again, Madre?" she cried eagerly. "With the beginning of our flock why not make a beginning of the fiesta of the shearing?"

"We shall make a beginning," Doña Leonor promised. "Next summer, I trust. Happiness is medicine for us all."

Mother was always livelier when they were away from the house for a while. This morning Tia Nina had been in one of her fretful moods, and Doña Leonor's lips had folded tighter and tighter.

Lucia should be growing more sedate, Tia Nina had complained. She should be learning the stately demeanor of a lady. She should be made to wear the various boards and leaden plates that proper Spanish señoritas used to keep their figures trim and flat. She should be made to keep her complexion delicate with fruit pastes and powders.

When Doña Leonor did not reply to all this, but only bent her head lower over her work, Tia Nina burst out still more peevishly: "Of course, Leonor, if you wish to spoil your daughter completely, with all this hoydenish freedom, it is your own affair."

At that Doña Leonor looked her sister-in-law in the eye and answered evenly, "Yes, Nina, you are quite right; it is my own affair."

Tia Nina's brows shot up and her mouth popped open, but before she could voice her angry protests, Doña Leonor continued quickly, "You will excuse me now, sister. I must go and see that all goes well with the shearing. Daughter, come with me, if you please."

So they had escaped. At first Doña Leonor walked rapidly, her face tense. Then she let out a big sigh. "Your poor Aunt Nina!" she said. "No children of her own, and none of the gaiety she loves. And not even the dainties she craves. We must be tender of her, Lucia. But God grant we may some day be in a home of our own."

Doña Leonor relaxed, and Lucia began to skip like a lamb. When they reached the shearing place, she dashed about boyishly, and Doña Leonor did not reprove her wildness.

They found Juan doing the actual work, with Gaspar helping wherever permitted, and Domingo shearing a single sheep, so that he might say he had taken part. The sun was bright and the air sweet, and Lucia thought contentedly that it would be like this—only growing more and more delightful as the flock increased—when they had their own rancho and could always give free rein to their spirits. If that dream would only hasten to come true!

"I want to shear a sheep myself!" she cried.

Under his bristling brows Old Juan shot a questioning glance at his lady. She nodded.

"It is one thing to be a young lady in the City of Mexico," she explained, "and another, I think, to be a young lady on the frontier. Whatever your occupation, my daughter," she added, "you can still retain the modest deportment that custom requires. And perhaps we should all be able to do what needs doing, in this dear, wild land of ours."

"I suppose my sister may one day need to run like a rabbit," Domingo commented teasingly. He had been watching her with an expression of half-irritated admiration, thinking perhaps that with all those heavy petticoats she did well to be so graceful and so fleet of foot.

"Running like a rabbit might save me my life some day," Lucia retorted.

Meanwhile Old Juan had seized the nearest sheep by one hind leg and brought it hopping to him. Gripping it with a deft hand above the hock so that it was harmlessly paralyzed, he threw it and held it for Lucia.

Pushing back her hair and breathing fast, Lucia tried to slide the great blades of the shears close to the skin as she had watched Juan do: close but not too close. It was far harder than it had appeared, but presently she felt the satisfying bite of the steel through the fleece, and widened triumphant eyes at Old Juan, her nose twitching in and out until her brother burst into laughter. Lucia's hair fell across her face again, and sweat prickled out all over her and ran from her nose and her chin like tears, but she persisted until she had undressed her sheep. Finally she folded the fleece as she had seen the men do, and put it with the others.

"Ho!" Domingo taunted. "Look at Lucia's sheep! One would hardly know it had been sheared!"

"Ho!" sang Lucia. "Look at Domingo's buck! He is wearing red polka dots from the nicks my brother gave him!"

"Very-very small nicks those," her brother declared loftily. "And if they had hurt the beast, would he not have mentioned it?"

Lucia watched her fresh-sheared ewe shake itself and go capering away as if its new lightness threw it out of balance and made it giddy. "It is their not mentioning it that makes me feel so funny," she said. "They lie so helpless and silent, with their mouths tight shut."

"And as for the nicks not hurting them, young master," Old Juan put in, after listening with his lips working ferociously over his toothless gums, "pray do not be too sure. And if it were not for this blessed country where there are so few stinging flies, I should have to watch every small wound and smear it well with pine tar."

"To heal the hurts?" asked Lucia.

"To heal, and also to keep the blowfly from laying her eggs in the opened skin," Old Juan answered.

Lucia flashed a complacent glance at Domingo. He might be Tia Nina's favorite, and Old Rosa's, but Lucia had always been preferred by Old Juan, just as she was by Tio Melchior. Up until now, however, Old Juan, though polite in his way, had treated her as if she were a child: more, a woman child, and therefore of the least possible importance. That was the way her uncle regarded her, indulging her when he was in a good humor and scolding her when in a bad one.

Today Old Juan had addressed her as if she were a person. She thought it must be because she was interested in the flock, and because she appreciated Plata's fine points. Old Juan did not merely herd the sheep as a job for which he was hired; he loved them. They had a lot more sense than folks gave them credit for, he often muttered, more sense than some señors and señoras he might mention.

Feeling wild and free and happy, Lucia ran here and there through the bushes and yucca and pulled from spikes and thorns every wisp of wool that the sheep had left there while they grazed. Before Doña Leonor called her to walk back to the house she had a double handful, and she waved the salvaged fibers gaily at Old Jaun, who stood watching her.

"There would not be so much as that if the browse were better, Missy," he said. "The healthier the animal, the tighter it holds its wool."

"It is like your orphan lambs, Lucia," her mother commented approvingly. "The menfolks will seldom bother with the criaturas, nor will they trouble to collect the stray bits of wool. Yet the orphan lambs may start a flock, and the tufts of wool in time can stuff a pillow or weave a blanket."

"Mother, I want to learn to spin and weave. Could not Gaspar teach me?"

Doña Leonor regarded her daughter thoughtfully. "It is not customary for our young ladies. Yet what harm? I myself have never liked to embroider day after day. And since Gaspar is himself a beginner, and works slowly, you might perhaps acquire the skill by watching him."

As soon as the shearing was over, Gaspar set about building a loom for use on the hacienda. He had managed to snatch an occasional hour from his regular tasks, and these he had spent in the convent, learning from Fray Antonio. The padre had brought a loom from Mexico City, and with his own hands he had made others like it, contriving the heddles and reeds from cords and wooden rods. He had fashioned the bobbins, like little boats, and the battens, to pack close the woof threads as they were woven; and he had made stick spindles, with their disks of well-smoothed wood near one end.

Gaspar followed the padre's example, working tirelessly with axes and knives, the only tools at hand. Sometimes he lugged home a weathered old viga that had come from a house abandoned at the time of the Revolt and left to fall to pieces. Such lumber, already dressed and well seasoned, was a treasure.

Doña Leonor, coming one day with Lucia as she often did to watch him work, stood staring at the partially made loom and then moved toward it, closer and closer, as if fascinated.

"What is it, madre mia?" Lucia asked in surprise. "What do you see?"

Doña Leonor laid her hand on one of the large end timbers and stood for a moment unable to speak. "These—these letters—J—G—A—R—José Gabriel Anastasio Rivera. An-no Do-mi-ni 1675. Gaspar, where did you find this timber?"

As much astonished at her mother's reading the inscription

as at her emotion, Lucia stared questioningly from Doña
Leonor to Gaspar. She was in time to see a concealing curtain draw across his face. It was as if suddenly he grew
stupid, or lost his usual easy understanding of the Spanish
language. Her mother repeated the query.

"The timber? I find him in the woods," he answered at
length, his hand describing a vague circle.

He went on fitting together the parts of the loom, using
wooden pegs in place of scarce and costly nails, or wet rawhide, which shrunk as it dried and made a fastening to out-
last the centuries.

For a few moments Doña Leonor watched him in contemplative silence. "Perhaps the Pueblos dragged it away and
later discarded it," she murmured.

"Why are you so concerned about it, Mother?" Lucia
inquired. "And how would my father's initials come there?"

"Oh, my Lucia!" her mother answered brokenly, "this
was one of the vigas in our own sala. Its ends rested in beautiful carved corbels, and this inscription—with his own
hands your father made it, may he enjoy peace."

After Doña Leonor had crossed the patio to the sala,
Lucia still sat thoughtfully regarding Gaspar as he worked.
Her mother had suggested to Tio Melchior and Tia Nina
that the former dining room might well serve as loom
room, since the sala was being used for meals. With its windows and doors throwing it open to view, she or Doña Nina
or Rosa could easily keep an oversight of the weaving. Lucia
could sit on the sill, as she was doing now, and watch Gaspar chop and pound and fit, while she held in her lap the
smallest and weakest of her orphan lambs, dipping her
fingers into a jar of goat's milk at her side and letting the
little thing suck.

Gaspar rested briefly from lifting and holding the clumsy

timbers, and gazed at the carved letters and numerals. As he regarded them, he ran one slim brown finger over the initial *J*, swept it down the stem and swung it round the curly tail.

"Hotah," Lucia softly named the letter. "*J*, for José, for Juan, for jardin."

Gaspar's eyes glinted at her through his thick, straight lashes, and he spoke softly as she. "Hotah. Para Juan. Para José. Para jardin. Para—" He glanced at the earthen jar into which Lucia's fingers were dipping—"para jarra, Señorita?"

Delightedly Lucia widened her eyes at him, and made a roguishly long lip that twitched down her pert nose. "For jar!" she agreed, nodding emphatically.

"Hotah!" he repeated, drawing it carefully in the air. "Hotah para la jarra."

"Now!" Lucia exclaimed. "*G*, hay. That comes next on the viga." She watched him trace it with an intent finger, and then sprung her surprise: "*G*, para Gaspar."

Gaspar flashed her a look so deep with satisfaction that Lucia caught her breath. He wanted to learn to read. He wanted it so much as that. She blinked, and he frowned at her in quick alarm, so that she sniffed back the impending tears and spoke hastily.

"I was remembering when I began to learn my letters. I could think of nothing else. But I could not tease Tio Melchior into having me taught. He had found the signing of his name about all he needed, and he thought learning was foolish for girls. Besides, he says, people can make trouble for themselves by book learning. A governor of New Mexico and his lady were held for years by the Inquisition, and partly because they read books."

Gaspar was listening, bemused.

"Domingo taught me," Lucia concluded. "At siesta, when everyone else was sleeping. Reading—it seems something much more than just—reading," she ended lamely, and gave herself again to feeding the lamb.

Gaspar returned to his task of setting together the carefully cut pieces of the loom, and as he worked he murmured, "Hotah, para la jarra—Hay, para Gaspar, and—para—gozo?"

Once more Lucia laughed with pleasure. "For joy! Yes, Gaspar! And now take that next letter, like my two hands with the finger tips together and the thumbs across. It is *A*—ah."

Without pausing in his work, the Navajo youth looked from Lucia's small tapering hands to the carved letters and said, "*Ah*. For what, Señorita? For Ana?"

"Si. For Ana. And Anastasio. And arroyo." She gestured in the direction of the chasm to the eastward.

The warm summer morning mounted toward noon as Lucia sat thus in the comfortable shade of the portal. The lamb finished its milk and slept. The loom stood ready for its warp threads. From the kitchen, through the zaguán, came food fragrances. Stooping, Gaspar marked on the earthen floor with his knife, murmuring letter names and words as he did so; drew the numerals and spoke them: "Uno—seis—siete—cinco: one—six—seven—five."

"You are very-very quick, Gaspar. You learn faster than I did. But I think," she suggested, "that you would do well to turn that viga over so that Tia Nina cannot see the carving. She would be scared to death to think that you had taken it from the old hacienda. 'The haunted hacienda,' she still calls it, even though Fray Antonio has blessed the place."

Gaspar neither denied nor admitted that he had fetched

the beam from the lost hacienda. But one of his infrequent, shining smiles narrowed his eyes to slits and broke whitely across the dark bronze of his face.

Next morning Lucia went early to the loom room, while Gaspar was busy with other tasks. The loom was set up with woolen warp, and the end timber showed the yellow of freshly cut wood. Either Gaspar had replaced the old viga, or else he had hewn off the carved letters with his ax. Lucia felt sorry that she should not see it again; and her mother was sure to mourn the loss.

Lucia spent some minutes flat on the floor beyond the loom. With a knife she scratched on the clay the letters of the alphabet, deep and large enough so that Gaspar could see them as he worked.

So throughout the month of June, Lucia continued to nurse her lambs on the threshold and watch Gaspar. Her voice, soft and light and whispering as the leaves of the cottonwood, and Gaspar's, murmurous and deep, were lost in the gentle noises of casa and patio. The loom pedals clacked; in the kitchen just beyond the wall Soledad made the air vibrate as she beat the chocolate to a foam or clap-clapped the tortillas between her palms, her frail little baby at her side. The bare feet of Old Rosa and Lupe thumped ponderously, thudded swiftly, as they prepared the comida. Above, in the willows and cottonwoods, cicadas wove together the fabric of sounds with their high shrill song.

By July several things had grown out of these quiet mornings. Two of Lucia's lambs had died, but four had grown big and strong enough to be let out with the flock, all bearing on their ears the tiny nick that was Lucia's mark of ownership. Gaspar had learned the alphabet and could read many words that Lucia scratched for him on the clay floor.

And Lucia had carded all the wisps of wool that she had from time to time harvested, and had spun them, together with more that Doña Leonor gave her.

Gaspar had made cards for Lucia. They were like those the Indians used, when they used cards at all, he said, blocks of wool with strong, stout cockleburs set in them, to comb the fibers smooth for spinning.

Gaspar made her a spindle, also, and showed her how he had seen a Navajo woman use one. He sat on the ground, kicking off his sandals, and angled his legs sidewise with the soles of his feet turned up. Then he held the tip of the spindle between his toes while he twirled the stick and drew out the fluff of wool, which he had affixed to the spindle with a few firm twists.

Lucia imitated him closely, until Old Rosa came waddling from the kitchen with a clay saucer in her hand, grunting her disapproval. Old Rosa said it would be more seemly for Lucia to do it her way, with the tip of the spindle resting in the saucer on the floor. Lucia did it Rosa's way when Rosa was present, and the Navajo way when Rosa was gone.

For a long while she could not catch the knack of twirling the spindle, twisting the wool, and drawing it out, all at the same time. Then, suddenly, she had the trick, and felt as if she had won a battle. She learned to retwist until her yarn was reasonably strong and even, and then she made it into skeins as Gaspar did, reeling it from hand to elbow. She washed it with yucca root, as Old Rosa showed both her and Gaspar, and finally she colored it. Some she dyed with pigweed, for the pink she liked so well, and some with indigo, brought up in lumps from Mexico. By this time, rewarding her perseverance, Doña Leonor had given her enough wool to weave a blanket for her own bed.

By midsummer still another thing had happened. Gaspar

had built a second loom, and this one was for Lucia. When Lucia saw it, she fell speechless with surprise and gratitude. And noticing that one of the endpieces was of wood more weathered than the rest, she ran inquiring fingers along its underside.

Yes, the old inscription was there. Gaspar had removed it from the first loom and kept it for Lucia's. She smiled her gratitude. Her stammering "Muchas gracias!" could not express her thanks.

Chapter 10

Crash!

DAY followed day, that summer of 1695, with no rain for Santa Cruz, no rain for the whole region. Sometimes a bank of heavy clouds swelled and spread, and the hearts of the Riveras swelled with it. But always the clouds scudded swiftly across the sky, clutching their precious burdens, and bestowing no drop of them on the thirsty land. The corn curled its yellow blades and died. Except for the cactus, which hoarded water thriftily in its succulent leaves, even the wild flowers of the region bloomed meagerly. In consequence, few butterflies and bees were to be seen.

On San Juan Day, June 24, Fray Antonio made a procession through the fields, with his altar boys and a train of settlers. Since the resettlement, Santa Cruz had celebrated none of the fiestas except the villa's own Day of the Holy Cross, which fell in early May. For St. John's Day they left their work and bore, on a canopied platform, the statues of the Virgin and Child, and of San Juan, imploring them to look upon the dying vegetation and send rain. Even then no rain came.

Fray Antonio privately remarked to Domingo, who was studying rhetoric with him, that this might be God's punishment for the Spanish treatment of the Pueblos. Domingo asked him why, then, the Tanos, the very Indians whom they had driven out and up to Chimayó, had no more rain than Santa Cruz? Fray Antonio said sternly that it was one of the inscrutable mysteries which they should not seek to divine. But then he laughed and admitted that the question had been bothering him too.

The Rivera household diligently searched meadows and hillsides for green things that would make food, though they had to be cautious about going far from the village, since the Indians were so generally unfriendly. Rosa knew how to prepare and cook the roots of the milkweed and wild onion, and the little potatoes that were the roots of the cattails. She made greens of the tall, purple-blossomed bee plant, and of pigweed and horsemint and mustard. She watched the milkweed and yucca pods, to gather them young and tender for cooking.

Everyone kept close watch of the sparse clusters of chokecherry in the region, to pick them before other fingers or beaks or claws should snatch them away. They watched also the wild plum bushes. The sight was maddening, for the fruit set, and grew as large as Domingo's thumb, turned a lovely pink-purple with a frosty bloom—and dried up and dropped without ripening.

"Perhaps the wild grapes higher along the stream?" fretted Tia Nina. "Perhaps the cultivated grapes of our people, up Chimayó way—or their peach trees. Let us not entirely despair of fruit. Let us look toward Chimayó, where our grapes were famous long before the Revolt."

The Riveras were eating a thin meal after the siesta, Tia Nina dolefully scraping the last flavor of spiced chocolate from her cup.

Domingo chased a crumb of biscoche round his plate, frowning. He felt as if he had eaten nothing all day. Besides, he was torn between pity and irritation whenever he looked at his aunt. Her round face had sagged a little, and it began to show wrinkles as she lost a few pounds through the forced reduction of her diet. Though he chafed under her coddling fondness for him, like silk ribbons tied too tight round his wrists, yet he was, in a measure, bound by it.

"I will hunt up and down the whole valley, and set the seal of the Riveras on every abandoned grapevine and peach tree," he promised her banteringly.

Doña Leonor shook a decisive head. "We will do without fruit rather than have you risk Indian arrows and spears for it, my son."

"Oh, to be sure, to be sure," Tia Nina fluttered. "I did not mean Domingito. But why not send Gaspar?"

Lucia cried out angrily, "It would not matter if Gaspar were to stop an arrow, Tia Nina?"

Doña Leonor said, "Daughter!" Tia Nina said, "Well, I am sure, Señorita!" Domingo said nothing, but thoughtfully nibbled his nails.

That afternoon he and Gaspar rode along the melancholy little stream to inspect the rabbit snares they had set. Fernando had also showed Domingo how to thrust a rough stick deep in a rabbit burrow and twist it until it tangled in the rabbit's fur, then jerk it out. Lucia cried for an hour when he brought home his first catch, alive but half-skinned. Uncle Melchior laughed and said it was just like a woman; Gaspar looked at her as if puzzled by her grief, and Domingo said huffily that they must all go hungry if they were to look upon wild beasts as people. Yet he caught no more rabbits that way. Today the boys found several of the scrawny little things in their snares, and dropped them into a saddlebag. Rabbits were not very good eating at this season, but meat was meat, and Rosa's spices and fixings would make an edible stew of them.

"We will go a little way up the valley," Domingo said. "We can see if the old grapevines are still alive, and whether they have set any fruit. The peach trees, likewise."

Gaspar made no reply, but prepared to follow. Giving Oro the lightest touch of the spurs, Domingo turned his head up the gently rising road that led toward the settlements at Chimayó. Gaspar's ugly gray ambled along half a length behind.

The way followed the little river, and passed the ruined orchards and crumbling house walls of abandoned haciendas. Without irrigation, the trees were dead or dying. Now and then the boys spied one that had sent out its roots to the stream and thus survived, showing green leaves amid its smoky tangle of dead branches, and a few wrinkled immature peaches. The elder Riveras had described the past beauty of this valley, a green skein curving along the hillside, and threaded with silver by the little irrigation ditches of the early settlers. Now it was a melancholy remnant, like a sheaf of dead flowers on a grave.

There were few signs of life. It was as if the birds and beasts had fled from this sere land to more fruitful regions, as the butterflies and bees had done. And the boys rode for a mile, for two or three, without meeting a human being, although Domingo had an uneasy sense of presences lurking behind cottonwoods and willows, or in hollows on the hillside, or amid the great rocks that bordered some of the old haciendas.

"Gaspar, do you feel as if there were Tanos watching us?" he asked, as much for the relief of hearing his own voice as for Gaspar's opinion.

Gaspar grunted noncommittally. Glancing around at him, Domingo saw that he was soberly scanning the ravine.

"Maybe we should turn back," Domingo said, tightening his reins.

"Maybe yes."

They were already wheeling about when Domingo caught sight of a ruinous arbor that still half-supported a grapevine of a thriftier green than they had seen before. "Look, Gaspar!" he cried, forgetful of his own uneasiness. "Let us see this closer before we go."

"Don Domingo!" Gaspar cried out in alarm.

With eager spurs Domingo was urging Oro along an old trail toward the vine. At his companion's warning shout he glanced back. In the same instant the earth rose cracklingly around him and struck head, shoulders, breast, legs, with shattering force.

Racking pain shocked Domingo out of oblivion. No longer in the crushing embrace of the earth, he was being shaken like corn parched in a kettle. Thud-thud, thud-thud-thud, sounded a rhythm of blows beneath him, and every thud shot fresh pain through his body. He pulled open protesting eyes. What was this?

He lay across the gray's shoulders, in front of Gaspar, who was crouched protectingly above him. Domingo had a blurred sight of Gaspar's dark set face and of blue sky with white clouds flying backward away from him. Then his eyes swam shut again and he saw nothing more, felt nothing more, until he found himself gazing up at a herringbone pattern of red and blue. He lay blessedly still and safe in the softness of one of the home colchones.

Staring around him, he tried to push himself up. Doña Leonor and Doña Nina and Lucia were all hovering there, ready to thrust him gently back. Even more effectual were the throbbing pains that completely possessed him.

He turned his head in a feeble attempt to escape the wet rag that Tia Nina was tearfully applying. "What happened?" he demanded.

"We do not know," his mother said. "Gaspar came galloping home, he and the horse all in a sweat and you across the gray's shoulders."

"Looking more dead than alive," Tia Nina blubbered, determinedly pursuing his face with the dripping cloth.

Lucia leaned over her brother and spoke in an earnest, loud voice, as if he were deaf. "He said, 'A Tanos horse trap!' That was every word Gaspar said: 'A Tanos horse trap.'"

Domingo lay arranging this in his pain-racked head, and his brow knitted with remembrance. "Verdad! True! But—Oro?" he demanded, struggling up on his elbows. "Where is my poor Oro? He crashed into that plagued pit like a stone from a catapult. Was he killed? Was he?"

"Lie down, my son," his mother said, thrusting him back firmly, while Tia Nina sniffled more noisily, and sloshed water desperately over him and the pillow. "After all, we must thank the good God that it was the horse and not you. So far as we have been able to discover, you have not even broken any bones."

"And, look!" Lucia's eyes were sparkling with excitement. "One of these was sticking in Gaspar's saddle, and the other in his shirt." "These" were two long arrows.

"But the point of that one is stained!" Domingo exclaimed, his eyes focusing with difficulty.

"It barely grazed the lad's shoulder," Doña Leonor assured him. "I dressed the scratch myself, to make certain."

Hot pain was whirling through Domingo's head. "Call Gaspar," he begged. "I must see for myself. And I want to ask about Oro."

Old Rosa, who had been sniffling almost as loudly as her mistress, went waddling out of the door, shouting as she went, "Gaspar! Oh, Gaspar! The young master desires you!"

Domingo shut his eyes and listened impatiently while her calls died away in the kitchen, while they sharpened again, while her daughters' voices, and the children's, took up the cry. As on the day when the Navajo woman had escaped, Rosa soon waddled back, shaking her head, puckering her face, shrugging her shoulders and waving her hands.

"He is not here. He is not with Old Juan. The gray is not here, either."

"Why is it growing dark?" Domingo inquired in sudden alarm. Were his eyes wounded by these knives of pain that stabbed his head?

His mother's reply at once reassured and amazed him. "It is evening. You were long unconscious, my son," she answered smiling at him shakily.

"We have had no cena, no, not a morsel!" Tia Nina spoke solemnly, clasping her plump middle with one arm and fanning herself with the other hand, while her eyes rolled piteously upward. "Rosa, now that all is well, do prepare us our supper. We shall then feel as if the world were right side up again."

Domingo lay with closed eyes, thinking that all was not well, so long as Gaspar was away, nobody knew where; and Oro, his own little golden pony, like enough dead. The names chased themselves round and round in his head: Gaspar—and Oro—and Gaspar—and Oro—and Gaspar!

Before supper was set on the table, Domingo heard above him a quiet voice: "Don Domingo. I, Gaspar."

Domingo's eyes popped open and looked up into Gaspar's. Even in his shaken weakness he realized that those eyes held an expression he had never found in them before. For the moment, the usual curtain was drawn aside, and warmth and tenderness looked out.

"Your shoulder? Is it really all right, Gaspar?"

"It was nothing. And you, Don Domingo?"

Domingo grimaced. "Only bruised and sore as if a hundred demons had beaten me with rods. No more. But my horse? My Oro? I suppose he was killed when he went plunging into that abominable trap?" He held his breath, awaiting Gaspar's answer.

"I thought he would at least break a leg," Gaspar said. "I could not wait then to see. I went back afoot. I got him out. He was cut and lame. But alive."

Domingo was up on one elbow, staring incredulously. "Surely you did not get him home?"

"No. But as far as the tower. I took him inside. Left him there to rest."

Tia Nina was crossing herself and making the sign for

the evil eye with finger and thumb. "The witch's tower?"
she cried out in horror.

"Fray Antonio says she is no witch at all," Lucia reminded her.

"No witch," Gaspar echoed stolidly. "And she know
what to do. She brew herbs. Bandage his legs. Bathe
sores."

Domingo shut his eyes so that nobody should see how
warm and strong was his gratitude. "You are good,
Gaspar," he mumbled. "But you should not have risked
yourself. Not for a horse. No, not even for Oro."

Next day Domingo was sorer still. All his hurts had
stiffened, and each time he moved they felt as if they
were breaking. His head whirled, and pain scourged it
unless he held it motionless on the pillows. Fray Antonio
came to look him over and suggest additional treatment.

Fray Antonio was wise in the ways of sickness and
wounds, as in almost everything else. "You will be as good
as new, my son," he assured Domingo. "I trust you will
make a novena, when you are well, in thanksgiving to God
and the Virgin for your escape from death."

Domingo spoke soberly. "Thanksgiving to God and the
Blessed Virgin and Gaspar."

Fray Antonio's smile warmed. "True, my son. A faithful friend, Gaspar. My daughter," he interrupted himself,
looking toward the door, "why are you weeping?"

Soledad was standing in the portal, waiting, while the
tears slipped from her swollen red eyes. "It is my baby,
Padre. She grows no better."

The padre rose quickly and followed her, excusing himself to the Riveras as he went.

Gaspar also had evidently been waiting outside. As
soon as the padre had passed into the servants' courtyard,

the Navajo youth came in, bowing respectfully to Don Melchior, who sat in the embrasure of a window, contemplating his nephew.

"You have seen Oro? How did you find him?" Domingo asked eagerly.

"Like you," Gaspar replied, a glint of humor in his dark eyes. "Worse than yesterday. Worse also than tomorrow."

"Thank you, Gaspar." And then Domingo's words rushed out like a stream long dammed up by this and that. "Gaspar, I have been thinking. Now, while I am recovering from my mishap, now would be a good time for me to teach you your letters. And when I am well I could perhaps take enough of your work so that you could attend Fray Antonio's classes. Uncle Melchior, you will not forbid this, when Gaspar saved my life, no less?"

Uncle Melchior grunted sourly. "You may live to regret it."

"Thank you, tio mio!" Domingo said, as fervently as if Don Melchior had given full and free consent. He felt happy and free, like one who has overcome a long sickness. Ever since Fray Antonio first suggested that Gaspar should be taught, Domingo's selves had fought for and against the idea. Against it because he feared the hard work of tutoring a primitive; and because his uncle was sure to be vexed with him for suggesting it, even if he did not forbid him outright. Against it, too, for a reason he did not admit even to himself: if Gaspar learned to read, would he not soon reach a mental equality with Domingo? Yet against these considerations Domingo had all the time fought for it: because Lucia was in favor of it; because Fray Antonio, whom he loved and admired, had suggested it.

So now he spoke gaily to Lucia, "Sister, have we something that would show the letters?"

Demurely, with bright, expectant eyes, Lucia brought him the only book in the casa. It had been one of their father's treasures, that volume bound in gold-tooled leather.

"Sit you here on the colchon beside me, Gaspar." Domingo spoke breathlessly. "Now see. Here is the first letter of the alphabet." He pointed at a large, ornate initial *A*, and waited for Gaspar's puzzled wonder.

Gaspar gazed soberly. "Yes, Don Domingo," he said gravely. "It is *ah*, is it not? *Ah*, for Ana, for arroyo, for abaco."

The room was so silent that the buzz of a fly sounded like an explosion. Domingo looked incredulously at Lucia. She covered her mouth with her hands. Tio Melchior was staring under knitted brows. Gaspar bent closer above the book, as if wholly engrossed in seeing the letters, but Domingo fancied that his lips were twitching.

Gaspar's finger descended on the letter *B*, as if he had been searching for it through the maze of looped printing. "*Bay*," he said. "For bello. For banco. *Say*"—he touched a *C*—"For caja. For calle. And, if Don Domingo please, it says here, 'The — knight — led — the — horse — ' "

A snorting giggle erupted from behind Lucia's hands, and the reading stopped. Domingo's finger shot out toward his sister. "You!" he stuttered. "Y-you little imp, you have been teaching him on the sly."

She had done it again. He, Domingo, had put the idea into her ready mind, and then, while he dillydallied, she had rushed to do the thing he was debating.

"Tio Melchior," he said hurriedly, not giving himself time to argue, "as soon as I can be about again I will do enough of Gaspar's work so that he may have two hours a day, maybe, with Fray Antonio. I find that my pupil is already promoted beyond my teaching. Will you give your permission? Will you, tio mio?"

When his uncle hesitated, Tia Nina interrupted, blubbering. Tiptoe with the wonder of Gaspar's book learning, Lupe's Cleofas had fetched her from the kitchen where she was tasting Old Rosa's cookery.

Tia Nina whimpered, "Say he may, Don Melchior, querido! Say you will permit it. Did he not save our Domingo from certain death?"

Lucia reënforced her aunt's words. She came and took her uncle's hand in the coaxing way she kept for him, running a little finger tip along its blue veins, making her mouth like a kiss and gazing at him from melting eyes.

"Oh, very well," he said, tapping Lucia's chin with a heavy forefinger. "Who am I to oppose the will of the whole family?"

After siesta next day, when Gaspar came with news of Oro's progress, Domingo had the book ready for him.

"Read a little, my student," he said. "Then I will read aloud awhile. This is a great story."

It was *Don Quixote*, and Lucia clapped her hands at the thought of such entertainment. The rest of the household were as pleased as she. The ladies fetched their fancywork, and Lucia got out hers. She had begun to embroider a colcha, and was heartily bored with the prospect. The cover of one of the mattresses had worn too thin for use, and Doña Leonor had replaced it with new cloth. That left a fine large piece of the old linen for embroidery, since nothing that cost so much effort and time as hand-woven cloth could be wasted. When he had read a page to the admiration of the assemblage, Gaspar brought his spindle and sat a little removed from the Riveras, spinning.

Domingo read well and with liveliness. Occasionally he interrupted himself in a passage of drama or humor by flinging out an expressive arm, or by throwing back his head to laugh. Then he would utter a heartfelt "Aye!" at the twinge that marked every movement of his bruised body.

Gaspar appeared completely uninterested in the story, completely absorbed in his spinning. Yet once when Domingo was reading about the shackly horse, and how the gentle lunatic knight named it Rosinante, Gaspar uttered a deep chuckle.

Coming from him, the sound was so startling that Domingo stopped in the middle of a word, and Tia Nina cried, "Ay de mi!" and clapped a dimpled hand to her heart.

Lucia said, in a voice shaken with giggles, "It is very-very funny, no? To name him Horse of All Horses, that rawboned, moth-eaten nag!"

Gaspar said, "I think it is a good name for the gray."

And at that remark everyone laughed in good earnest.

It was not till the reading was done for the day and Tia Nina and Doña Leonor had gone to direct the servants about the comida, that Gaspar pulled a folded paper from the pouch at his belt. While brother and sister eyed it curiously, he opened it and held it toward Domingo.

Although it was yellow and smudged and split along some of the folds, the writing on it, and the lines drawn across it, had remained distinct. With Lucia puckering her brows at it over his shoulder, Domingo studied the words.

"North—East—South—West," Lucia read aloud, impatiently brushing the hair from her eyes. "And Domingo! At the corner it says—"

Domingo pulled the paper out of her reach. "It says, 'Entierro de—' And that is absolutely all it says. 'Burial place of—' Gaspar, how did you come by this? Where did you find it?"

Gaspar's lips motioned eastward in the direction of the haunted hacienda. "From Dinneh woman."

"The witch woman?" Lucia gasped.

"Where would the Navajo woman get it?" demanded Domingo.

"Whullah?" Gaspar replied with a shrug. Then he translated the Navajo into the Spanish. "Quien sabe? Who knows? She bring from hiding place. Today, when I go see Oro. She say, Give to Lady Leonor or childs. First I think, No; witch business. So I start to burn it. Then I see the writing. I read." Intense pride lay in those words. "I read," he repeated with dignity. "So I bring."

"Hush!" cautioned Domingo, slipping the paper between the leaves of *Don Quixote*, his eyes on the door.

Tia Nina was returning, babbling over her shoulder to Rosa.

"Do not say a word about this," Domingo murmured, his cheeks burning with excitement. "We will keep silence until we can look into the matter ourselves. It might refer to valuables hidden at the time of the Revolt. Many things were concealed then: money, plate, other treasure. We will keep silence."

Chapter 11

A Change of Weather

DOMINGO had not doubted that he could go to the old hacienda within a few days and talk to the Navajo woman. Whenever he and Lucia were out of earshot of their elders, they resumed their discussion of the unfinished chart, if that was what the paper was. Burial place of what? And where?

It might refer to any one of a hundred localities. Nuevo Mexico was always turning up maps or coming upon signs of buried treasure, or of rich mines that had been lost when the owners were driven away. Everybody had his own story of fabulous hidden wealth, told him under oath of secrecy by the nephew of the brother of the man who had found it

and lost it again, or hidden it only to forget the hiding place.
The Navajo woman's paper might even have come from a
distant section, since her tribe wandered over a wide expanse
of country.

However, it was more probable that it had originated
hereabouts. Lucia was sure it had.

"Without a doubt it came from Santa Cruz or from this
very Valley of the Neighbors. Myself, I believe it came
from our mother's old ranchito. Else why should the Navajo
woman have told Gaspar to fetch it to Mother?"

"And pray how would the Navajo woman know that the
ranchito had once belonged to our parents?" Domingo
inquired sarcastically.

Lucia blinked at that, but did not back down. "I would
wager my lambs," she vowed, her blue eyes deepening to
violet as the pupils dilated, "that the paper indicates something that was buried by our own father, may he enjoy peace.
And what would he be most likely to bury? Maybe the giant
crucifix from Spain: ivory and ebony, our mother says, and
very-very precious."

"Or the family silver," Domingo agreed, taking fire from
her. "The table silver that was our father's pride."

Lucia spoke almost reverently. "Plates for the dinner,
hand-hammered from purest silver, almost too heavy to
hold. And forks. And a silver cup for each. And the great
water pitcher."

"Let us not encourage ourselves until we have learned
more about it," Domingo counseled his sister in an elderly
one, though his cheeks still burned. "It might be as you
say, yes. It might be 'Entierro de la plata.' But there are a
hundred chances that it might not, to one poor little chance
that it might."

He twitched with impatience to set about the inquiry, but

the days dragged on past any delay that he had expected, and he remained still bound to house and patio. When the swelling of the rest of his bruised and battered body had subsided, his ankles and lower legs remained oversized and darkly discolored. Fray Antonio examined the areas with gentle fingers and pronounced the injuries sprains rather than fractures. Yet when Domingo brightened at the diagnosis and tried to heave himself to his feet, the padre laughingly pushed him back on the divan.

"At least three weeks more, my son," he said. "Have patience. You are safer, besides, in your own patio. I do not like the look of the Tanos, these days."

Domingo's face grew hot at the implication. "I am no longer a child, to be coddled, Father," he said stiffly. "Does fear of the Tanos keep you within the walls of Santa Cruz?"

"They, too, are my children," Fray Antonio answered serenely. "What were the words of Fray Juan Pio just before his Indians killed him? 'My poor children, I would give a thousand lives for you.' Danger does not drive a father from his sons and daughters, especially when he feels that these sons and daughters have suffered grave wrongs. Up to this time most of us who came to win the souls of our red brethren have been granted the eternal glory of martyrdom. For myself I expect nothing else."

Domingo drew a quick, protesting breath. "Father! They could not kill you who have done so much for them!"

Fray Antonio smiled, but left the protest unanswered. "With you it is different. You build a new world here on earth. You will need all your strength and quickness in the hard years that stretch ahead," he said, with the solemnity of a prophet. "You must not stiffen these ankles of yours by using them too much and too early. Exercise them carefully, yes, but go far afield, no."

So Domingo had to subside and content himself within the patio and the small walled garden west of it. Soon he was able to limp, with two sticks, as far as the portal of the loom room, where he could watch Lucia and Gaspar at their looms. Oftener he sat and read aloud from the marvelous tale of *Don Quixote*.

That was a pleasant time, between siesta and supper, in the drowsy afternoons of late summer. Reading was entertainment, and the new country was barren of entertainment. Only when couriers came up from Old Mexico, or when a wagon train labored through, was there meager word from the outer world. And, except for the padres and De Vargas himself, there were few men in all New Mexico who had had an education or travel, so that they knew anything beyond the simple and restricted happenings on the frontier.

Even Rosa's grandchildren came scampering to join the circle when el señorito began to read. The smallest ones squatted on the clay floor of the patio, playing busy little games of their own; the two-year-old cousins, Chiquita and Ramon, and four-year-old Felipe. Five-year-old Femie listened, understanding a sentence here and there. Lupe's Francesquita, who was eight, had tasks to do, shelling beans or chick peas, and her ten-year-old sister Cleofas knitted like a veteran. They worked and listened, and their eleven-year-old brother, Miguel, sat on his heels and stared at the reader with his mouth hanging open and his great dark eyes bemused with the tale.

Rosa would grind pecan meats from Mexico on a heated metate, so that they would melt enough to blend with the spices and the chocolate that she ground and mixed with them for the favorite drink. Lupe carded or spun or did any one of a dozen necessary tasks. Soledad would perhaps work with the soap which she made from kitchen fats and lye, while her poor mite of a baby lay and stared blankly toward the sunshine, too frail even to play with its own clawlike hands. Soledad would soak the soap and mix it with ground rosebuds and other fragrant and medicinal leaves, flowers and roots, and make it into cakes for the ladies to use on their faces. Again and again she paused to brush the flies from the baby's face, or turn her to a more comfortable position.

Roque and Fernando were as much interested in *Don Quixote* as were the others, and did their best to find quiet occupation within range of Domingo's voice. There was plenty of handwork needed to make the house inviting and homelike again, and there was, besides, the need to fashion furnishings and adornments for the new church, though Fray Antonio did not drive the men at the task as some padres were said to do.

Roque and his father before him had been taught by the priests in Mexico to tan leather soft and pliable and then paint it with rich color for use as door curtains and table covers and many other things. Fernando was especially deft at fashioning wooden spoons and ladles, plates and trenchers for the table. Between them they were making a bulto, a figure of one of the saints, for the villa church, Roque preparing a stiffened cone of leather to serve as the lower part of the body, draped in a concealing costume, and Fernando carving the upper part and having an anxious time with the face.

Domingo and Lucia regarded Roque and Fernando with affectionate contempt. They were mestizos, part Spanish, part Indian, whom Soledad and Lupe had married in Mexico City, mild, kindly little men, but timid as rabbits. Both had been well taught and followed their crafts diligently as long as Rosa had her eye on them. During the reading, Fernando's knife moved slower and slower on the pine knot he was shaping into a bowl. Finally he stopped entirely, his eyes fixed on Domingo's face and his mouth hanging like his son Miguel's. Roque, who was even more fearful of Doña Nina's reproof, glued his gaze on his leather. Yet his hands, likewise, worked more and more slowly, until they were stilled, and all Roque's spare body was tense with listening.

Lucia, perched on the wellcurb with her embroidered colcha, stole mischievous glances at the two men, and then bent lower over her work, holding in her mirth till Domingo came to something funny in the book, to give her an excuse for bursting into laughter. Sometimes her pursed lips would not hold it back, and it would explode in a wild, unladylike whoop.

Even embroidering was not dull when Domingo read aloud. As on a sampler big as a bed sheet, she had embroidered letters across the top, spelling out her name and the place and date, and weaving round them rows of flowers and leafy vines. As the reading went on, she grew more ambitious, and put in animals. First she put in Oro, and Rosinante, and her uncle's prancing black stallion. She added the oxen that pulled the carretas and the plows, Raton, the burro, and Chepe, the sheep puppy. Finally, she embroidered the sheep, a whole line of them.

When Domingo closed his book on the day's reading, Doña Leonor laid aside her knitting and inspected her daughter's handwork.

"Lucia," she exclaimed, "this might be fine enough to serve as an altar dorsal for the new church."

Domingo leaned sidewise to look. "What are the animals?" he teased. "You had better put their names under them, Sister, if you do not want us to take a horse for a rabbit."

Lucia tossed back her hair and made a face at him. Tia Nina waddled over from the mattress where she had been resting, and bent above the colcha.

"I am sure," she argued with her nephew, "anyone as smart as you ought to be able to make out which is which. You can easily tell the ones that are horses. By their colors and by the men on their backs. Men would not be riding rabbits, I hope. And the oxen by their horns and by the carretas. To be sure, the burro's ears might well be horns, though that is no matter, for anyone would know that an ox would not be wearing saddlebags. There is only one matter that is not perfectly clear to me. Why does this lamb have a crown on his head, Lucia? A sheep with a crown—well, I must say!"

"It is because he is Plata, the prince of our flock," Lucia explained. Domingo's teasing and her aunt's backhanded compliments hardly troubled her, since her mother was so genuinely pleased and surprised.

"I believe," Lucia murmured, suddenly shy about it, "that I will make a border of the flowers and animals. All the way round. Then in the center—How would it be to have the Virgin of Guadelupe and the peon Juan, to whom she revealed herself?"

"Ay de mi!" Doña Nina exclaimed. "You aim very high, Señorita!"

So *Don Quixote* turned Lucia's colcha into a work of art instead of the piece of drudgery it had started out to be. Yet she liked weaving better than embroidery, for when she wove she did not have to sit still. Her feet flew as fast as her fingers and relieved some of her pent-up energy.

Her impatience had kept her from respinning her yarn

enough to make it uniformly fine, so her first blanket had a rough texture. "But it is lovely," she declared candidly. "It is really very-very lovely."

On its creamy white ground, stripes of pigweed pink alternated with stripes of indigo blue, both outlined with brownish black from the few black sheep in their flock. Old Juan always kept a few black and a few red sheep. Their wool helped the weaver, saving some of the work of making dye and coloring the yarn. Lucia would not have wished to use only those natural tones, for she found it as interesting as it was laborious to hunt the plants that made rich, permanent colors, and to prepare them. Lucia's colcha, likewise, required all sorts of hues, and to make them herself was like creating something out of nothing: soft green and yellow and orange, and reddish brown and pink and rose and blue.

One day Old Juan came to look at her weaving and her embroidery, with its frame of flowers and animals slowly growing and the space in the center left blank for the great adventure of the peon Juan and the Virgin. Old Juan stood with his hat under one arm, wordlessly studying Lucia's work. Finally he scratched his head till his wild hair stood out more wildly, and grinned affectionately at his señorita.

"Before you are done you will have to make another picture of that Plata, bigger and with bigger horns, he grows so fast," Juan said. "But I would know him anywhere, Señorita. By the brown spots. And it is good, since you like to use the black yarn, that two of our twins last spring were of that color. Next summer you can use their wool."

It was not primarily for the weaver that Old Juan always kept a few of the dark sheep, but for help in count-

ing his flock. When the flock scattered out over rough
ground and Juan wanted to be sure they were all in sight,
he counted the black ones he could see. If all five black
ones were there, it was likely the ninety-five white ones
were likewise. When the flock should grow to a thousand,
to ten thousand, then the black ones would be still more
valuable as counters.

It would take years to reach a thousand at the present
rate, for the flock was doing poorly this dry season. But a
drought must break sometime, Juan argued. During late
August and early September he had taken his charges
farther up, on the edge of their summer range, though the
danger of Indians, which at first had kept him on the winter
range near at hand, had grown no less. On the contrary,
the Tanos waxed more sullen with every rainless week
that passed. When Doña Leonor protested against the
risk Old Juan was taking, he replied stubbornly that the
creatures might as well die by the hand of Apaches, or
by the teeth of coyotes, bears and timber wolves, as by slow
starvation. Already they had almost cleaned up the sparse
herbage on the lower range, and what would happen to
them come winter?

Old Juan's curved stick and slingshot were kept busy
these days, for coyotes and lobos were bolder, and Chepe,
though responding well to training, was only half-grown,
and no match for his wild cousins. As for Gaspar, he was
kept busy in other ways.

As winter came on, the household would need more
blankets and more jerga, the heavy woolen cloth used
for carpets and mattress covers and clothing. So Gaspar's
shuttle raced with the hurrying year. And he had all the
hunting to do nowadays, and must go farther and farther
away to keep the kettles filled with meat. Domingo and

Lucia were uneasy whenever he mounted his new-named gray, Rosinante, and set off alone.

One day in late September he did not return until long after the early dark had fallen, and he met anxious reproaches from Domingo, Lucia, and Doña Leonor, and even from Doña Nina. He had promised, she reminded him fussily, not to go farther than San Cristobal Pueblo to the southeast, and not to venture again in the direction of Chimayó. He was their sole defense at home, she scolded, with Don Domingo still crippled, and Don Melchior scouting the country, and Roque and Fernando scared of their own shadows.

Without attempting an excuse, Gaspar silently indicated the wild turkeys and antelope he had brought. Even next day, when he and Lucia were weaving and Domingo was watching them work, he continued unusually silent.

Domingo was passing on to his sister and the Navajo youth some of Fray Antonio's lessons in the geography of the new land. To the northward and eastward, he said, stretched unmapped country, hostile with Comanches and Apaches, with Utes and other wild tribes whose names he had not yet learned.

Buffalo swarmed through that wilderness, huge horned beasts with curly wool, which Domingo and Lucia knew as yet only by hearsay. One of the excitements of their father's day had been the hunts that the young Spanish organized, riding out beyond their hills to the country of the buffalo and killing great numbers for their meat and hides. Uncle Melchior said they would have more such hunts when the Indians took less of their time.

The region to the west was better known. There, many leagues away, the Moki lived, in villages resembling the pueblos in New Mexico, and southeast of them the Zunis, famous for their precious lake of salt. Farther west and north in the vague distance lay the ocean. Some exploring padres had penetrated to this western coast, where the weather was always summer. There they hoped some day to build a great string of missions, and convert the Indians to Christianity and teach them the arts of agriculture, wine making, and sheep raising.

"That is all that is known of Norteamerica, even by our wise padre. But you are not listening, Gaspar!" Domingo interrupted himself, looking up from the vague map he had been scratching on the earthen floor.

"No," Gaspar admitted.

"And of what are you thinking?" Domingo inquired stiffly.

"The Tanos. They grow uglier."

"Well, and did we not know that already?"

Lucia was crouching on the floor, her chin in her hands and her eyes fixed on the map. Now she shifted her gaze to Gaspar's face and said, "Gaspar, you have learned something new!"

Gaspar's peddling foot lifted a long line of warp threads, and he sent a bobbin of soft green wool sailing through between the sky of warp and the sea of warp. His eyes followed it with sober pleasure. The Indian looms had no bobbins, and no mechanism for separating the warp, and Gaspar enjoyed the greater efficiency of this Spanish method. Not until the bobbin had reached the other side did he wet his lips with his tongue and speak.

"To San Cristobal I came. After dark. And mingled with the people. There are many Dinneh who do not love the Spanish. So the Tanos did not fear me. They plot."

Lucia gulped. "What do they plot, Gaspar?"

"To attack the settlers. Not yet at Santa Cruz. At the lonely haciendas."

"Is—this a lonely hacienda?" Lucia stuttered.

Gaspar shook his head as if he did not know what to answer. "I had believed that with Don Melchior—and with our guns—"

"We must tell Fray Antonio," Domingo said.

They did tell the padre, when he came to inquire about his patients next afternoon. Fray Antonio sighed. "I am not surprised," he said. "If there were something definite, I would send a courier to the governor-general, to ask him for more soldiers."

Gaspar spoke. "I will go again. To San Cristobal."

"No, my son," the padre forbade, decisively. "I will find some other way to get information. But now I must hasten back to Santa Cruz. A heaviness is in the air, and a heat, that may bring moisture. It promises some sudden change, if I know anything of New Mexico skies and atmosphere."

That night, before he went to bed, Domingo stood in the portal, looking up into the sky. "For once," he said to Lucia, "I believe the padre is wrong. Only see how bright the stars are. If tomorrow is like today, I will ride up to the summer range to see Old Juan and the flock."

Though Oro's legs were stoutly bandaged, he was by this time scarcely limping.

In the night Domingo was roused by a furious wind. The house hugged the ground too close for the gale to shake it, but even through the thick walls Domingo felt a deep tremor. Around the tight windows sounded the whistle of the wind, the rattle of twigs and the crash of tree limbs. Domingo raised himself on one elbow, blinking sleepily.

Stars and moon must still be shining, for light flickered through the mica panes. He twisted about to ease his aching ankles. Old Rosa had said last evening that the renewed pain in his joints was a warning of weather changes, and it was true that the air was colder. Yesterday had been too warm for fires in the corner fireplaces, but now the sala, where he slept, was chilly. He pulled the heavy woolen blanket over his head and drew up his arms and legs till he was warm enough to sleep again.

He was wakened next morning by the slow, heavy pad of Rosa's feet on the floor, and by the crackling and spitting of fragrant piñon and juniper wood as they burned. He had been so tightly curled that not only his ankles but his whole body ached. He uncoiled, peered out, and then sat up in surprise. Windrows of fine snow lay on the floor beneath the windows and at the door, those nearest the fireplace beginning to melt.

"It has snowed?" he demanded of Rosa. Snow was still a pleasant novelty to him. He could not remember any during his years in Mexico City, and in the two winters since they started up toward Santa Cruz, it had not become commonplace.

"Truth, it has snowed," Rosa grumbled, pushing a knot of fat wood where it would catch, and shivering violently as she spread her hands to the blaze. "Truth, it still snows. Sometimes I could wish that we had never come back here."

Already under the screen of the blanket, Domingo was pulling on his clothes. Half-dressed, he went to the door and opened it a crack. A gust of wind leaped through, wrenching it from his hand, banging it noisily, letting in a flurry of fine flakes. Through the thick white curtains of snow that swirled in the air, he was not able to see across the patio. He slammed the door shut.

"Caramba!" he cried. "A change of weather indeed."

His mood of happy excitement persisted until the breakfast came in, carried by Rosa's daughters. Close on their
heels came the rest of the Riveras, all muffled in serapes
even for the short dash along the portales from their sleeping rooms. Lucia's face was puckered, and her nose was
doing its exercises, drawing in as her mouth pulled downward.

Watching her in some surprise, Domingo politely wished
his elders good morning and then demanded, "Sister, what
ails you?"

"The snow!" Lucia wailed.

"Me, I like the snow," he protested.

"Yes, but Silver! Silver and my other lambs. And the
whole flock. And Juan."

Domingo's high spirits flattened. "They are still on
the upper range?"

"It may be that Old Juan had brought them down. He
is weather-wise, Old Juan." Yet, though Doña Leonor
spoke soothingly, her face was deeply troubled.

"Let us send Roque or Fernando out to see!" Lucia
cried.

Tio Melchior stood before the fire rolling a cigarette.
He spoke deliberately. "Until the violence of this storm
subsides—" He took out his silver lighter, with its roll
of cotton and its slow-burning punk, applied it to the
cornhusk, drew on it till the cigarette was lighted, while
Domingo and Lucia waited for the end of the sentence—
"until its fury lessens, it would be sending good money after
bad, to send Roque or Fernando or Gaspar after the flock."

Lucia gazed at her uncle with frightened wet eyes.
"But—Old Juan—" she quavered.

"Come, come, hijita," her uncle said, blowing out a

pennon of blue smoke, "Old Juan knows how to look out for himself in any weather. Wherever he finds himself he can throw up a shelter. And, as to the flock, he will do for them all that can be done."

A few minutes earlier, Domingo had been ravenous. Now, as they pulled up to the table, he found that his appetite had departed. Only Tio Melchior and Tia Nina did more than pick at their food, a most unusual state of affairs since their diet had become so meager.

All that day the wind roared round the house, tearing off twigs and branches and hurling them against the windows and on the roof. Sometimes it shook out a vast sheet of snow, as a woman might shake her apron at the poultry. Sometimes it drove the snow down the chimney, where it hissed on the burning logs and brush. Sometimes it rushed in this direction for a minute, then veered on itself and rushed the other way, as if trying to catch its own tail.

When Roque or Fernando fetched more wood for the fire, they scurried in, serapes over heads, pulled shut the door, stamped the snow from their feet on an old rug, and deposited their load, breathing noisily. Every two or three times, Rosa swept up after them with a grass broom. Tio Melchior impatiently rolled and smoked one cigarette after another, and the two señoras also smoked, until the air was blue.

At length Tio Melchior muttered that he would step across to the stable and see that the horses were all right. Horses were both few and precious; the Comanches and Apaches were especially bold and crafty about stealing them, and the loss of a horse crippled a soldier, here on the frontier.

Tia Nina cried, "Oh, mi alma, no! Do you forget the

storms of the old days? Things of terror! Men lost and frozen to death fifty yards from their own door—"

"I cannot get lost here in the patio," said Tio Melchior, with a shrug. "With buildings or an adobe wall on all four sides, and the gates still barred as they were for the night."

When he had gone, Domingo took out his book, and they passed the morning reading, with Gaspar presently bringing his spindle and sitting on the floor to spin and listen.

All day the snow whipped blindingly around the rancho, shutting it in from the world outside. Then in late afternoon the wind at last fell weary, and the snow dropped lazily, straight down.

"Can we not send out now to look for Old Juan and the flock?" Lucia begged her uncle.

He was sitting in the big carved elbowchair, his feet on the hearth, staring into the fire. Crouching on the hearth, Lucia gazed up pleadingly into his face.

"In the morning, I think," he said, with the half-smile that was about the best he could summon, even for Lucia. "So early a storm seldom prolongs itself. Tomorrow the sun will shine."

Lucia looked miserably from her mother to her brother, and both avoided her eyes. There was nothing anyone could do.

Next morning Domingo woke to a great stillness. The wind had died completely, and without opening the door he knew that the snow had stopped and the sun was shining. The light through the translucent window was even brighter than usual, because of the reflection from the white ground.

The snow was two feet deep on the level, and there were drifts as high as Domingo's head where the boisterous wind had heaped it against bushes or walls. Almost all the yellow leaves had been stripped from the trees, and large branches hung dangerously, broken by the weight of snow and leaves together. At all this wreckage the sun smiled complacently, shining so hot that the snow rapidly grew spongy and began to sink into the ground, and to run in bright rivulets down every slope, so that the air was filled with tinkling music.

"Gaspar can perhaps plow through to the winter range on his gray," Tio Melchior conceded at midmorning.

"And I with him," declared Domingo. "I am no more than stiff, and so also my Oro."

They set out, the horses mushing through the fast-settling snow, making good headway where the wind had cleared a stony ridge, and the next minute plunging to their bellies in hollows that had drifted full. The boys rode cautiously, Gaspar often jumping from his saddle to scout ahead, testing unfamiliar white surfaces with a long stick. It was well into the afternoon when they caught sight of Old Juan.

With a shouted greeting, the shepherd went on pulling at Raton's bridle. Head thrown up and long ears flapping back, Raton braced himself with all four legs, unwilling to follow his master into the treacherous depths. Finally he surrendered and came with a rush that almost upset Juan. In the saddlebags Domingo could make out two of the smallest lambs, doubtless Lucia's orphans.

Close behind the burro, Silver and Chepe led a line of grayish-yellow bodies that wound slowly down the path the sheepherder was making for them. Domingo shaded his eyes against the dazzle of sunlight on snow, and counted the black sheep. "Uno—dos—tres—cuatro. Four of the blacks. Is that how you make it, Gaspar?"

Gaspar nodded, speaking in his own tongue: "Din."

They were only a few feet from Juan now, and he heard them and shrugged disconsolately. "Truth. Four. When we have got these poor children to the corral and food, we must go back and fetch in the dead. El lobo y el coyote, they will go ahead of us unless we hasten. We must save the hides, since that is all we can save."

The sun was low when they brought the sheep into the corral. Old Juan had let them stop and browse on the willows and alders that grew in low spots along the way. They were perking up a little by the time they got home, and Silver even accomplished a feeble bounce as he entered the gate. Domingo laughed at that; it always amused him to see the sheep jump when there was nothing to jump over. Old Juan often slowed them up for counting by holding his staff across the open gateway, so that they must leap over it; after the first two, he could drop the staff, for the rest would jump as the first had done.

Doña Leonor and Lucia had heard the sheep bells and Chepe's barking, and were waiting for them at the corral. Domingo could see that they also were counting noses. Like her brother, Lucia laughed when Silver leaped in air at the gateway, but the laugh broke in a sob.

"Only—only four of my lambs left?" she gulped, scrutinizing the heads that bobbed along below the level of the adult sheep's.

Gaspar's lips shot out toward the burro's back, and Lucia managed a rainy smile at sight of two more of her orphans.

When the flock was all inside the inclosure, Doña Leonor said, "Eighty-one. We have lost about twenty, Juan? And you? Are you all right?" she added quickly.

Old Juan shrugged, grinning up at her like a gnome.

"Very-very well, Señora," he assured her. "Only very-very sorry that I could not keep the sheep safe."

While they walked through melting snow to the gate of the main patio, he related his adventure. He had started for the rancho the day before yesterday, not trusting the weather. Darkness fell, however, before they had come far, for they had been a long distance up among the hills. He wished to drive the sheep on through the night, being alarmed by this time, but the wind prevented him. Here on the heights it had blown a hurricane, and the poor scrawny sheep were distracted by it. It parted their light fleece and blew through to their skins, chilling them.

So he had made no headway before the snow began. It was driven furiously by the wind, and the sheep broke and ran before it, all following one silly buck. For once Juan could not stop them, and they piled up in a dry wash, one climbing senselessly on another's back till some had suffocated. Even after the snow had stopped, in the morning, and Juan had started them homeward in single file, a few more had been lost. One had fallen from weakness and had been unable to get up again. Juan, warned by the bleating of her lamb, went back after her, but too late. As he arrived, a buzzard swooped and struck, and the ewe was dying when Juan drove the ugly creature away.

"If they had been well conditioned," Juan finished, almost blubbering, "they would easily have survived so short a storm. Señora, I finished off that last one and bled her well, so that we can use her, at least, for food." He motioned to Raton's back, where the carcass was slung.

"You have been faithful, as you always are," Doña Leonor commended him with a forced smile. "I am thankful that you yourself have suffered no harm, Juan."

Yet as they went on into the patio she spoke sorrowfully. "We have lost half the gains we had made. At this rate, when will our flock amount to anything at all?"

"At this rate, when can we return to a hacienda of our own?" she was doubtless thinking. Domingo was thinking it too, so busily that it was some minutes before he missed Gaspar.

"Why, where is Gaspar?" he demanded, when he had slid stiffly from Oro's back.

"He went back after some of the carcasses. He is yet another faithful servant," Doña Leonor observed.

"These last weeks he has been more like a brother," muttered Domingo.

Chapter 12

At the Mouth of the Kiva

GASPAR came in that night after darkness had fallen. He had brought in a few hides, and dragged home several carcasses to be skinned at the rancho. One was the body of a lamb born overlate for its own good, too tender to survive the early storm.

"Its wool is still fine and soft and curly," Doña Leonor said. "Roque can tan it for the bed of his ailing little one. Nothing keeps a cradle so warm and dry."

Though still heavy with a sense of loss, the Riveras were relieved to have all their household safe at home. Moreover, they could sleep soundly, since the wind had ceased battering house walls and roofs. When Lucia poked her nose out next morning she found the air as balmy as in June, washed clean of dust, and with bright streams still running along the patio walks. She hurried to the edge of the portal and stood sniffing the autumn fragrance. Snow and wind had almost stripped the trees, and most of them lay on the ground, breathing out a sharp, strong scent. Yellow as gold against the intense blue of the sky, a few still clung to the tips of the cottonwoods.

"All the flowers are blighted," mourned Lucia, as her brother crossed the portal and stood beside her. "They are turning to black rags, and that old sky is laughing at them. Now that the flowers are all dead, I suppose we shall have summery weather right through November."

"Too bad," Domingo said absently. "But the snow will give the sheep more food for a while. And hark to the cocks and the hens. They are shouting for joy." His voice trailed away and he stood frowning across the service patio.

Lucia's gaze followed his. Through the open zaguán she could see Gaspar, skinning one of the dead ewes, and Roque, smiling as he contemplated the pelt of the curly lamb. Roque would soon have it pegged down in the east courtyard, covered with cooked sheep's brains. In the same way he would soften the flesh side of a silky goatskin and the other sheepskins, so that they could be used for rugs before the colchones. When Roque was done with them, washing and scraping, washing and scraping, they would be flexible and white.

"What makes you look so glum?" Lucia asked her brother. "I see nothing but Roque and Gaspar—"

"It is Gaspar—his forehead," Domingo muttered.

The sunlight blazed on Gaspar's head. It made his

hair shine with blue high lights like a raven's breast, and it set aflame the *R* branded on his brow.

"But it is no different from always, brother. Why—?"

"Lately it has seemed so much worse," Domingo answered harshly. "Maybe because—lately—he has been so much more a person. Not 'just an Indian slave.' A person."

"Since he saved your life up Chimayó way? Isn't it funny that saving your life would make him love you? I would have expected it to work the other way: make you love him."

"Who says I do not?" Domingo said roughly. "When it is Gaspar I can see reason in Fray Antonio's queer notions. The padre thinks we have no right to capture or buy Indians and own them as if they were sheep."

Rosa and Lupe were carrying the breakfast through the zaguán from the kitchen, and the smell of hot spiced chocolate drew the brother and sister into the sala. Lucia, though she consumed her share of the food, gazed absently before her, while Domingo chatted with their uncle and ate ravenously.

"What are you planning today?" Tio Melchior asked his nephew, sitting back in his elbowchair and sipping the thick chocolate from his spoon.

"I ride up to the summer range and see if there are more sheepskins to salvage."

Tio Melchior laughed grimly. "You will find nothing to salvage, unless perhaps a little wool for spinning. When last I crossed the patio before retiring I heard El Coyote and all his brothers singing up yonder on the range, and El Lobo joining in." His voice sharpened. "Do not go alone. Those rascally Tanos—"

"Gaspar will go with me," Domingo assured him. "I

am no child myself, and Gaspar is shrewd as well as strong."

It was then that Lucia broke into the conversation. "Tio Melchior," she cried, "will you not set Gaspar free? Gaspar—he should not be a slave. He is as smart as Domingo, I think; and certainly as good."

Tio Melchior's eyebrows shot up in astonishment. "Child, what kind of ranting is this? Why do you not ask your brother to give Oro a slap on the withers and set it free?"

"Gaspar—Gaspar is a person," Lucia stuttered indignantly. "Please, oh, please, Uncle mine!"

Tio Melchior struck the arm of his chair a mighty blow. "Lucia," he bellowed, "let us hear no more of this. I am a poor man. To set Gaspar free would be like pouring pieces of eight into a quicksand. Especially now, when he has grown to usefulness. If you want him freed, buy him from me, my fine señorita. Once he is yours you can do as you like."

Don Melchior pushed back from the table, his chair grating on the clay floor, and glared at Lucia under his folded lids. She straightened her shoulders and met his stare with a frightened smile.

"How—how much did he cost?" she faltered.

Doña Ana, she recalled vividly, had bought an Indian captive for two fanegas of corn, four blankets, six yards of cloth, four knives and a plug of tobacco. But Domingo had said that their uncle paid in pesos.

"How—much did you pay?" she repeated.

Don Melchior looked amazed at her persistence, and laughed unpleasantly. "Fifty pesos. But that was two years ago."

"Fifty dollars of the land?" Lucia asked in a tiny voice that shook with fright. Even she could not take Uncle Melchior's bad humor lightly.

"Hah! So you catechize me, Señorita!" he roared. But his face softened as he looked at her, sitting straight and small, mouth buttoned tight and blue eyes fixed on him unblinking. "You should have been a boy," he said, and then added, not to weaken too much, "so that I could take the rod to you as you deserve. Your father would turn in his grave if I were to whip his girl child."

Still Lucia waited.

"Fifty dollars of the land, yes. I suppose it would be easier for you to get those than fifty dollars of silver?"

Lucia looked at her brother for support. Domingo was scowling down at his wooden plate and would not give her a glance. She turned questioning eyes to her mother. "I could sell my lambs——"

Even Doña Leonor failed her. "The lambs are yours, yes," she said gently. "But how should we ever build up a flock if we let our lambs go? No, I could not allow it."

For a moment Lucia sat wretchedly silent. Then, with a murmured excuse, she pushed back her stool and ran out into the courtyard to find a place where she could cry unseen. Her brother presently followed and found her. He stood poking at the moist clay with his boot toe.

"You get such wild ideas, Lucia," he grumbled.

Lucia stared over her shoulder in amazement. "But—it was not my idea. It was yours. Such a thing would never have come into my silly head. All the same, I knew it was true as soon as you said it."

"What did I say?"

"About Gaspar. It is true, brother. He is a person."

Domingo reddened under her earnest gaze, and wetted

his lips. "We have no money," he growled. "I suppose you would want me to sell Oro."

Lucia considered. She knew very well that he could not sell his horse. A mount might make the difference between life and death, between starvation and nourishment, in this wild country. "But I would want you to want to," she said thoughtfully.

"You are a funny little thing, hermana mia." His tone was grudgingly affectionate. "If you think a thing, then you must do it, de pronto. It is perhaps well that you do not have many thoughts."

At her puzzled face he laughed outright, and tried again, speaking like a teacher. "We go and hear a sermon by Fray Antonio. But does everyone expect to come home and do everything the holy man says?"

"Well, but why not?" Lucia inquired, blinking hard and knitting her brows.

"Why, why, it is simply not the way of the world," Domingo spluttered, waving helpless hands.

"The Padre Nuestro says, 'As in heaven, so on earth,'" his sister argued.

"Oh, you are hopeless!" Domingo cried, caught between laughter and frowning. "I can waste no more time talking nonsense with one who will not listen to reason. I must go and see to the work of the ranchito." And, putting on a superior air, he stalked off to saddle his horse.

Soon afterwards the two boys rode away, and a short time later a courier rapped smartly at the gate with a message for Don Melchior, who thereupon galloped off in a hurry, telling Doña Leonor to see that the gates were kept barred. An hour later the door in those gates was cautiously opened to Fray Antonio, who had jangled the bell commandingly.

He knew that Don Melchior had been called away, he said, striding in on sandals clogged with mud from the road, but he was disturbed to find the boys also gone. For a little while he sat silent in the elbowchair, gazing thoughtfully into the embers of the fire, by which he was drying the muddied hem of his robe.

"Father, you are troubled," Doña Leonor said. "Is there evil news?"

When the padre glanced around as if to see who else might be within earshot, Doña Leonor answered his unspoken question. "Doña Nina is in the kitchen instructing Rosa as to pastries. With Lucia as well as with me you can speak freely. I assure you we shall have no hysterics."

His gentle eyes blessing them, Fray Antonio nodded assent. "Perhaps the youth Gaspar has related to you the vague plottings that he heard as he mingled unnoticed with the Tanos? At San Cristobal not many days since?"

"Yes, padre."

"After the lad told me, I went and did some listening for myself. Three nights I crouched in the darkness near the mouth of the kiva—that antechamber of hell." The gentle eyes blazed—

"Padre, you should not have risked your precious life," Doña Leonor remonstrated.

He smiled, tranquil again. "I wrapped myself in a buffalo robe and waited afar off until the men were inside the unholy place. And, when I drew near, I heard black words—black." Shaking his head, he fell silent a moment. "So deceptive they can be, these simple-seeming Pueblos. Quiet and submissive and paying their devoirs to Our Lady like true believers, while their hearts devise our destruction."

Lucia hitched her stool closer to her mother's.

"You mean they actually might plot another uprising?" Doña Leonor ejaculated.

"Señora, they are plotting it. Whether they will hold together long enough to carry it to its conclusion, I do not know, of course. But I have sent a courier to the governor-general and put the matter before him, asking if we might not have a few more soldiers, the better to patrol the outlying haciendas."

Lucia held her breath, her eyes wide with hope, when her mother asked eagerly, "You have had an answer, padre?"

"An answer, Señora, but not a favorable one. De Vargas replies that similar rumors are coming to him from all over New Mexico, so that it would take a hundred soldiers to comply with the requests. And there are scarce that number in the whole kingdom, and they needed where they are. He says that any who are fearful for their lives may return to the greater safety of Santa Fe."

Fray Antonio paused, his eyes questioning.

Doña Leonor answered quietly. "No, we stay where we are, padre. This is our home and here we remain. How could a new country ever become established if its people ran away at every rumor?"

"I wish that Don Domingo were here, and Gaspar," the padre said soberly. "And I wish that Señor Rivera had not been called away. Are your menservants skilled in the use of firearms? And are they armed?"

"Roque and Fernando?" Doña Leonor's shoulders lifted delicately. "They are rabbits. We have two old muskets, but their rearward action is hardly exceeded by their effect to the fore. And Roque and Fernando would die of fright if they were ordered to pull the trigger. Old Juan, though, is another matter. He has courage. And since the blizzard he stays close at hand, keeping the flock near the corral."

"Use extra precautions, my daughter." The padre rose wearily and made the sign of the cross over them both. "And send me word if anything alarms you. I will go now and look at Rosa's youngest grandchild. They tell me that it will no longer take any nourishment, poor little creature."

Doña Leonor stood and watched him stride through the zaguán. "He is deeply disturbed," she said to Lucia. "We must see to it that the boys remain about the estancia until this trouble passes over."

When Domingo returned, he took a different view of the situation. "We must bring in more game while we can," he argued. "Rosa can dry any surplus for future use. Our uncle was right in saying that there would be nothing to salvage from the dead sheep left on the high ground; there were only gnawed bones. But from that height Gaspar sighted a herd of deer off to the west and south. We go tomorrow," he concluded firmly. "How long do you think one small mutton would feed our household?"

Not long, to be sure, for it was a small and spindling carcass, and Riveras and peones together numbered nineteen souls and eighteen meat-hungry mouths. Besides, the more savory the meat, the more quickly it vanished. Small and poor as the churros were, everyone admitted that their flesh was delicious, especially when studded with pearls of garlic and rubbed with other herbs that Rosa used so skilfully.

"Nevertheless!" Doña Leonor said, and folded her lips tight on the word.

Next morning Domingo did not appear for breakfast.

He was nowhere to be found. Rosa said, glancing uneasily sidewise at the ladies, that she had been awakened by stifled laughter before dawn, and had thought it sounded like Don Domingo and Gaspar. But she had heard nothing more and had fallen asleep again. And now both boys were gone, and Oro and Rosinante to boot.

It was evident that Domingo had decided not to wait for his mother to forbid him.

Tia Nina burst into tears at the news, but her sister-in-law said, "Why weep? The boys know the country and they know the danger. They will return."

She spoke so decisively that the other woman's crying quieted to sobs. Tio Melchior being absent, Tia Nina occupied his big chair. Her little feet dangled inches above the floor, and she sat with her little hands helpless in her lap and stared from swimming eyes at Doña Leonor. Gradually, reassured by Doña Leonor's quiet demeanor, she fell to eating again, and was comforted. But Lucia noticed that her mother stood often in the portal that day, listening, while the rosary clicked softly between her fingers.

Once she remarked composedly that the herd of deer had probably led the boys too far for them to return that night. "It may be several days before they come," she added.

Late that afternoon someone came home to the hacienda, but it was not Domingo or Gaspar. The bleating of sheep was suddenly shaken out across the stillness, and bells jingled. The household came running, came waddling, came toddling, out into the service patio. Old Juan was hammering at the gate, and, hearing his voice, Roque and Fernando ran open-mouthed and threw it wide.

"Help me—get them in—" Juan gasped. "Apaches!"

Chapter 13

The Siege

JUAN'S terrifying shout snapped the household into
action.

Roque and Fernando helped shoo in the sheep,
their voices cracked with fear, their bodies kept in the
lee of gate and adobe wall. Old Rosa seized the first weapon
that came to hand, one of the formidable iron door keys,
a foot in length, and waddled out into the road, snorting.
Doña Leonor leaped to her side, commanding Lucia to
stay where she was.

The sheep came pouring obediently into the patio, until
suddenly one changed his mind and circled back toward
the entrance. On the instant all that were inside veered

to follow him, and the courtyard was a dizzy, stifling whirlpool of wool.

"Santissima Virgen!" Old Rosa was wheezing, as she grabbed lucklessly at one sheep after another.

"Señorita! Plata!" urgently yelped Old Juan.

Obediently Lucia dived into the sea of milling bodies after her pet. He was so big now that she had to struggle for a grip round his neck. But after an instant's battle he came with a rush, earnestly trying to butt her out of his way. When Lucia went sprawling, he romped on over her across the patio to the far portales.

The nearer sheep tore after him, and soon the whole flock had swung round, splitting when they reached Lucia, and followed their leader. Before Lucia could gather herself up from the ground she heard the bang of closed gates and the clatter of dropped bars.

Tia Nina's loud wails accompanied the other noises like bad flute playing. Rosa was gasping out prayers as fast as her short breath would let her, and convulsively waving the mighty key. Old Juan alternately invoked the saints and shouted oaths at the sheep. Gradually the turbulence died like a waning storm, and Doña Leonor was able to make herself heard.

"Juan, have they followed? Or were they only trying to drive off the flock?"

Juan lifted his shoulders. "Quien sabe? Certainly it was the sheep they were after, and dead set to get them. Yet I do not think they would risk attacking the hacienda, unless—"

"Unless what, Juan?"

"Unless the Tanos who were with them had told them that today we were without men."

"Tanos? There were Tanos with the Apaches?"

"Yes, Señora. A sizable band of Apaches, and a handful of Tanos. Either hungry for mutton in this ill-fed autumn, or willing to vent their spite on us by helping to steal our sheep, those Tanos; or both at once."

Doña Leonor spoke decisively. "Then we must show the Apaches that the Tanos were wrong. We must show them that we have men."

Roque and Fernando began backing away at her words. They stopped as her clear eyes touched them and left them.

"Lend me a pair of your husband's breeches," she said, a hand on Tia Nina's shaking shoulder, "and a cape and hat. I can be a man as well as the next one. Juan, you and I will mount guard on the housetop. With yonder old musket."

She disappeared indoors, and soon returned, striding as boldly as long training in decorum would let her, and climbed one of the ladders that leaned against the house walls. Old Juan had already posted himself on the northeast corner of the roof, toward the quarter from which he had fetched his flock. Protestingly he looked at her over his shoulder.

"Señora," he muttered, "it is not fitting. Nor safe."

"What matter?" she replied brusquely. "And there is small danger, if we keep close watch. We must make them see that we have men; must make them see it well, before darkness falls. Then, when they have seen, we can settle ourselves behind the escarpments and watch through the canales."

"But, Señora, at any moment an arrow—" His voice trailed off and he stared past his lady with astonished eyes.

She swung around to see what it was that so amazed him. Lucia had stolen softly up the ladder behind her mother.

"You say yourself that there is small danger," the girl begged. "And when they see three men—they will think I am Domingo, will they not?"

She had pawed Domingo's best knee breeches and jacket out of the chest, and jerked them on; and she had found her father's old morion, which her mother had treasured. She had wadded her braids up under it, both to hide their length and to give more bulk to her small head; even so the hatlike helmet sat on her ears and she had to peer out under its brim. Doña Leonor's gaze swept down from the morion to the jacket sleeves, with the tips of Lucia's fingers sticking out, and to the knee breeches, which she was vainly trying to jerk up where they were supposed to be.

"They will think I am Domingo?" Lucia repeated, peering anxiously out under the helmet.

"They will think that Domingo has shrunk, then. But you are a good child, Lucia. Now, down! Since they must have seen that we are three men, let us take shelter. Creep over to the roof of the sala, Lucia, and watch to the westward."

They crouched behind the breastwork of the house walls, which rose three feet or more above the flat roof. The New Mexico houses were naturally fortified, with these breastworks pierced at intervals by holes through which wooden canales were thrust, to serve as waterspouts. Through these the watchers could see, and through them they could fire their weapons.

By this time the sunset had burned itself out, and the sky at the horizon was a clear, calm blue, almost, thought Lucia, the blue of the Virgin's mantle, as she meant to embroider it on her colcha. Above the blue rose a red-violet band, and over that a yellow almost as bright as an evening primrose. She wished that she could embroider a sky so beautiful.

A great star shone serenely out of the primrose, and through the softness of the Indian summer evening, the bells rang from the Santa Cruz chapel, silvery clear through the quarter-mile that lay between. Fantastic that anyone could be seeking to harm them on a night like this!

So thinking, Lucia straightened herself to move over to the next canal.

Zing! Zing! Zing!

She dropped flat with a thud, her body limp from shock. Arrows had whizzed past her helmet, struck the chimney pot behind her, dropped to the adobe.

"Sst!" Old Juan hissed angrily at her. "Your lady mother will send you below. Those Apaches—they have hawk eyes—"

Lucia hugged the rough clay of the roof with her whole body until she stopped shaking, and until the roaring in her ears grew still. Before those arrows zinged past, the attack had seemed hardly more real to her than one of Rosa's stories of the coco. She had even been able to think of embroidery. In a flash, everything was changed.

"We will use one shot. To show them that we are not scared," her mother said, steadying her voice.

Lucia lifted herself on her elbows and looked back over her shoulder. Doña Leonor was resting the muzzle of the old six-foot musket in the canal, and sifting a few grains of powder into its pan.

"Uno!" she said. "Dos!" She gripped the trigger that would snap the iron against the flint and send sparks into the priming powder in the pan. "Tres!" She pulled the trigger.

Lucia dropped her head and clapped her hands over

her ears, her eyes screwing shut at the bellowing roar of the old gun.

"Muy bien!" Old Juan congratulated his lady, when the echoing clamor left a dead silence behind it. "That will have scared them out of their skins. I will reload, Señora, that we may be in readiness." On his knees he crossed the roofs to her side.

Lucia twisted round on her stomach to watch. "I must know how. I might have to load it myself," she thought, shivering.

Juan put in more powder, and balls, and wool for wadding, and forced them all down hard with the ramrod which the musket carried on its back.

"Psst!" Old Rosa's eyes were peering over the inner edge of the roof, her fingers gripping the ladder poles. "Señora! Señorita! Are you safe?"

"De cierto," Doña Leonor assured her. "Rosa, send Lupe up with old carpets—with petates—the roof is still wet from the snow. But keep your head down. And see that you come by the ladder that rests against the kitchen portal. There you could hardly be seen from without."

"And mind the Señora well," Old Juan echoed sharply. "Too many have perished on their own housetops with an arrow through the head."

That was a long, strange night for Lucia. Except for the one shower of arrows, she would have thought that the Apaches and Tanos had not followed Juan, everything was so tranquil. The moon rose and flooded the roof with its calm light, making it necessary for the sentinels to keep well hidden. But there was no harm in talking, Doña Leonor decided, and it would help keep them awake as the hours wore on. She was so anxious to know exactly what had happened, that she called across the angle of the roof to ask Juan the story; but she deepened her naturally low voice to sound like Tio Melchior in case there were Indians near enough to hear. In that light air sounds carried far.

"Juan, how many sheep did they take?"

"Thirteen, Señor—Señora."

"Where were you? When they attacked?"

"About to get the silly creatures into the corral. With them inside and the gate fast, I might have held the Indians off with my slingshot. Maybe. But we were clean at the top of the hill when Maria warned us."

"Maria?" Doña Leonor and Lucia spoke the name together.

"The Navajo woman at the tower," Old Juan said. "Maria. Señora, from the first I thought she looked familiar. And now, when she called me, I knew without the shadow of a doubt. For she said, 'Mr. Mule Ears'!"

At any other time Lucia would have laughed at the outrage in Juan's voice. He had always contended that his ears were no larger than the average. Well, not much larger.

"But—Maria!" Doña Leonor breathed wonderingly. "I caught only a glimpse of the woman they called the witch, that day at New Town. But she was weather-beaten and old. Then I too must be old—"

"It was the proud walk and the proud high head that were so familiar. Maria always thought herself a kind of queen," Juan said resentfully.

It was clear that even in their peril Doña Leonor and Old Juan found Maria's possible nearness exciting. They were still discussing it when Lucia fell asleep. She slept and woke, slept and woke, to the murmur of their voices. Sometimes they were talking of the sheep and the Apaches.

"—how they dare run the risk!" Doña Leonor was arguing. "And how could they hope to get away with a band of sheep?"

"Señora, they dare anything," Old Juan muttered indignantly. "And when they are hungry enough they think nothing of slaughtering a few of us and making off with the sheep. As for getting away with them, they have it worked down to a fine point. With my own eyes I once saw them drive them into a column as long as this sala roof, with the strongest beasts in pairs on the outer edge, their horns lashed together. A string of Apaches ran on each side to keep them moving, and off they went, out of sight in a cloud of dust. As much as seventy miles they have driven sheep in a day. Little they care how the beasts suffer." He groaned at the idea, and fell silent, and Lucia drifted off into terrifying dreams.

She was roused by her mother's hand on her shoulder, and saw through blurred eyes that the sun was rising.

"Keep down!" her mother warned. "Old Juan is about to see whether the Apaches still surround us."

Completely awake, Lucia turned her head and watched Juan lift his ragged hat on his throwing stick, till the crown surmounted the wall. He jerked it down as a prompt covey of arrows flew over it. For a moment there was complete silence, and then Juan rested the musket in a canal and pulled the trigger.

Carefully he reloaded. "We have not much ammunition," he said. "If we had plenty of powder and balls, we could certainly hold out till help came."

"We have plenty of meat," Lucia said. Below them in the service patio the sheep were milling about, their distinctive odor strong in the nostrils of the watchers as the sun touched them.

"But not plenty of water," said Doña Leonor. "Even our well has been almost exhausted by this drought."

"Tio Melchior will be riding home any time, though, and Domingo and Gaspar."

"That is my greatest fear," her mother murmured. "Oh, Juan! Oh, my daughter! Keep the closest watch for our men!"

"But, Mother, surely they will be warned when they pass Santa Cruz. Surely the New Town has heard the musket."

"Yes, and said one to another, 'Someone shoots a deer or a turkey.' If they had thought otherwise, would not soldiers have come to our aid ere this?"

The picture of the Rivera men and Gaspar riding gaily into a trap tightened the tension. Otherwise, watching through the day would not have been too bad, since the Indians were most likely to delay any action till darkness. The sentinels were uncomfortable, of course. As the sun grew hot, the last puddles on the roof steamed dry. The breastworks and chimney pots gave scant shelter, and none when at noon their shadows dwindled to nothing. Lucia remembered a lizard, which long ago in Mexico City she had kept for a pet. She had forgotten it and left it in an earthenware pot in the blazing sun. *This is how it felt,* she thought now, and after all those years she wept again over the sufferings of the dead lizard.

Doña Leonor looked searchingly at her daughter's wet eyes and flushed face, and ordered her down to the sala for an hour's rest. She herself went for only a few minutes. How could she trust her post to anyone else, when it was her own son she was watching for? And, to be sure, Tio Melchior and Gaspar also.

The day had stretched out as if the sun had stuck fast

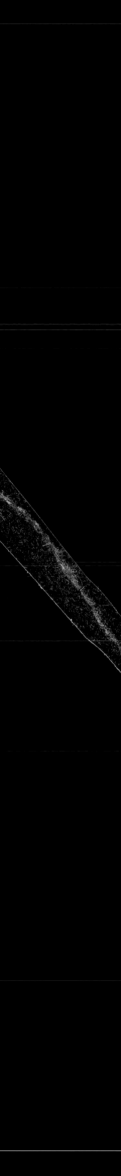

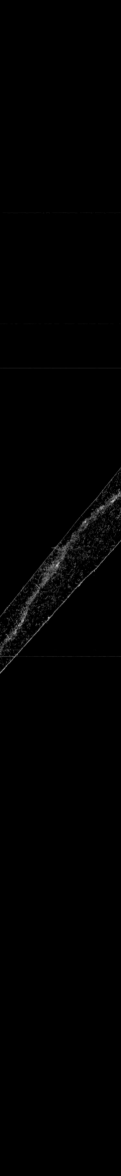

in the sky. It was incredible, on this timeless roof, that life could go on half normally in the courts below. The sick baby wailed thin and high, and the other children spoke out and even laughed sometimes, while their parents kept hushing them, kept herding them back into rooms that were twilight dim because Old Rosa had crammed fat wool-stuffed pillows into the few high windows that pierced the outer walls.

Incredible, too, that the Apaches should wait with such patience. They were not sure about the men, Old Juan guessed gloomily, believing perhaps that the señora and the señorita were Roque and Fernando and of no account. Undoubtedly, he added, they were making their own devilish plots to get the sheep with little cost to their own hides.

All this time no one had come along the road from Santa Cruz to knock at the barred gates of the estancia. To be sure, there were often days without passers-by.

Dusk did fall at last. "To have the sun go down and the coolness come so quickly, it is like drinking cold water when you perish of thirst," Lucia murmured.

"But it is these first hours of dark that I fear most," Doña Leonor replied.

Lucia gulped back cold new terror. "Because the moon will not yet be up? Because we might fail to see them when they rode in?"

"God protect them, yes," her mother answered solemnly.

"But if Juan is right, and the Navajo woman is Maria, she also will be keeping watch—"

"And if it is not Maria?"

If, when the darkness was too deep for the watchers on the roof to see them, if then the boys rode in, or Uncle Melchior—

Lucia's thoughts went on, shaken with this fresh panic. Then, after that, if all the ammunition had been used— Then, certainly, the hungry Indians would grow bold in the telltale stillness and swarm over the walls, swarm over the walls of the garden, perhaps, where the thicket pressed so close—

Or if those Indians were to hurl in balls of burning pitch, as they had been known to do—

And all this with Santa Cruz only a quarter-mile away

Lucia spoke through dry lips. "Mother, you must It is needful that you keep strong."

Doña Leonor eyed the trencher that Old Rosa had hour ago shoved along the roof toward her. She had look angrily at the tortillas and the joint of fresh-slaughter kid that Rosa had roasted. Food, she had seemed to say when my boy is in black danger?

"You cannot watch well without eating," Lucia persiste

Doña Leonor reached unwillingly for the trencher, wi the fat cooling white around the meat. "As soon as I a bit, you must go down and eat something hot and stret yourself, before night sets in."

Her mother's command was exactly what Lucia h angled for. The minute Doña Leonor finished her supp Lucia spoke again, her breath catching at the thought of th deed she planned. "Well, then, I go," she said, and wriggled backward to the ladder and down.

She ate in the kitchen, absently answering her aunt's tearful questions, while from every corner Rosa's grand-children stared wide-eyed at her and her male attire. The long hours of waiting had worn adult nerves thin, and Lucia noticed that improvised weapons were ranged in easy reach: enormous keys, and long-handled iron kettle holders, and metates that could deliver crushing blows at short range. With vague surprise, Lucia saw that her favorite oak batten was there, a formidable bludgeon.

As soon as she thought the dusk was thick enough, Lucia went out into the patio, wove through the mass of sheep, settling down for the night, and found Roque and Fernando, timorously looking to the poultry. "Come with me," she ordered them.

Exchanging frightened glances, they followed her amid the sheep, through patios and zaguáns, into the walled garden. Lucia stepped briskly, her back so straight that it buckled, to the corner which she had been watching because of the trees and bushes that pressed it from without. Here she turned to face the two servants, and spoke rapidly. For a moment they were silent, as if struck dumb by her words.

Lucia stamped her foot. "At once!" she commanded.

"But—little Señorita!" Fernando stammered.

"Aye, young mistress, the Señora will be so angry, so angry!"

"Me, I am angry already, this minute!" Lucia said breathlessly, stamping again.

Roque was wringing his hands. "Don Melchior—he will give us the scourge!"

"Better to be whipped than killed and roasted by the Apaches," Lucia threatened ferociously, backing against the wall to steady herself at the horrifying thought.

In the end they silently did as she bade them. Roque bent before her and she climbed—stiff from her vigil—on his hands, to his bowed back, and thence to Fernando's shoulders. From that height she was able to fling an arm over the top of the wall. With Fernando steadying her, she pulled herself up and lay across it on her stomach. For a minute, for two, she lay there, shaken from head to foot by the thunder of her heartbeats. Except for that thunder there was no sound save the endless music of the crickets.

Roque scrambled up beside her, lay flat, held her hands while she let herself down on the outside. Her knees hit bruisingly against the rough adobe, and her arms felt as if they were being jerked from their sockets. The shadows were so deep that she could not see what was below her.

"Let go!" she whispered, and fell into soft mud that spattered her to the hair.

Again she was tensely still, flattening herself against the wall and listening. No sound except her hammering blood, and the murmur of voices from the roof, and the common small noises of the thicket.

Lucia took off her morion and twisted her braids fiercely tight around her head. To be most effectively disguised, she should have cut off her masses of hair and let it fall loose around her ears, like her brother's. She jerked the helmet down hard over the braids, and then yanked it back so that she could see out from under. Then she stood backed up against the wall again, feeling as if her body were plastered to it, feeling that she had not the will power to pull herself away from it and push out into the terrible dark.

"Señorita!" Roque hissed fearfully.

She waggled a hand up toward him, her mouth too dry for speech.

"The moon will soon rise," he quavered in a voice that was barely audible.

Lucia drew a gulping breath, as if about to dive under water. Hands out before her, she went stumbling through the thicket in the direction of Santa Cruz.

Chapter 14

Blue of the Virgin

DURING those first few minutes, Lucia pushed on through the moonless night without a single clear thought to guide her. Fear filled her—shook her—devoured her.

The darkness of this underbrush was like the black of a windowless inner room, but instead of safe and solid walls to bound it, there were unknown treacheries. And within that shadowy circumference of danger, spiteful things tripped her feet, sprang out to assail her. Twigs had cat eyes to see under her helmet brim, had agility to reach in and sting her face. They caught at her clothing with malicious fingers. Twice they jerked off her morion, and

173

she had to stop and feel for it in mounting panic. The head covering was essential to her disguise, as well as a shield against enemy weapons.

In spite of her terror she progressed almost silently, stepping with the instinctive caution of the hunted. And soon her brain began to act again. *Once through the thicket that borders the garden walls,* she thought, *I can move faster. I can run. I must run, for if there are Indians watching the hacienda from this side, they will see me more readily in the clearing.*

Swiftly she wormed her way through the copse and paused at its edge, straining her eyes to pierce the darkness. The clearing was only slightly less black than the thicket, but a spark suddenly gleamed there and disappeared. It could not be a firefly; there were no fireflies hereabouts. It could not be animals' eyes; they did not gleam unless a light struck them. Lucia held her breath till her lungs seemed near bursting, as she waited for a reappearance of the glimmer.

The tense stillness was broken. Rat-tat-tat-whirr! crackled in her eardrums. Blind with terror again, she whirled about and crashed back into the thicket, hands out to ward off the punishing branches.

Before she had gone many steps, she forced herself to stop. Her noisy passage would betray her. The explosion so near her had been nothing more than the flight of a dove, alarmed by her presence. She knew the sound well, halfway between the rustle of dry cornhusks and the squeak of a rusty hinge. She stood still, pressing her aching ribs with both hands until she was composed again. Too late.

A hand fell on her arm, turning her blind and dizzy and weak, dragged her through the thicket and back into the clearing. She could see no one until another spark grew into many, and dimly lighted up a hand and arm holding a cedar-bark torch; lighted up her captor's buckskin shirt and partly shaven head. That brief, half-blind glimpse revealed that the man was an Apache.

The other, peering at Lucia in the glowing light of his torch, was not Apache; not Comanche; not Navajo. His grayish cotton garments announced him one of the Pueblos. More, his huge beak of a nose, curved in sharply at the tip, identified him as the San Lazaro Tano called the Eagle. Never before had Lucia encountered him, but Domingo had seen him several times, working sullenly around the church, and he had described him to Lucia.

These, then, were doubtless scouts for the war party besieging the estancia.

The Eagle was thrusting his pockmarked face closer to Lucia's. "Don Domingo!" he ejaculated, his eyes glittering in the torchlight. "Good!" he added in strangely accented Spanish, "We have captured the young buck."

Lucia's eyes wanted to close themselves and shut out his fierce, dark stare. Instead, she made a defiant effort and glared at him like a trapped squirrel.

The effect astonished her. The Eagle leaned closer—brought the torch closer—so close that it almost blinded her. His mouth fell open and he made the sign of the cross.

"Azul! Azul! Blue of the Virgin! Face of the Virgin!"

Gesticulating, he muttered to his Apache companion, who was holding Lucia by her elbows from behind. Relaxing his grip, the Apache craned forward to peer into her face.

In the momentary confusion, Lucia twisted her body out of Domingo's loose jacket and darted across the clearing. "Santissima Virgen volgame!" her heart was praying as she ran onward, fleet as a deer, and lost herself in the night. "Blessed Lord, give my feet speed!"

With every yard she made, her chances increased. The two Indians would not venture much closer to Santa Cruz and its sentries, always posted on housetops and in the corner towers. That realization, dim though it was, lent her strength, and she raced on till she reached the road this side of the villa entrance. The moon came up over the rising ground behind her, and sent out a quiet light veiled by trees and bushes. Now it was help rather than hindrance, letting her see, grayly, the way before her, the adobe walls looming ahead.

"Alto! Halt!" shouted a hoarse voice from the nearest tower.

Lucia stopped, lungs aching, mouth salty and dry. It was a moment before she could answer, and then only in a thin squeak: "I, Lucia Rivera."

"Who?" roared the voice.

"Lucia—Rivera. Help! Apaches!"

At once excitement—noise—hurlyburly. The church bell pealed long and loud, to alarm the whole countryside. Soldiers mounted their horses and thundered up the road. A few were left on guard, lest the hostile Indians might be using the attack on the hacienda to draw off the defenders of Santa Cruz and leave it open to a planned assault. Lucia stood listening and shivering before the chapel, with Fray Antonio and a group of the settlers who had been roused from early sleep. They heard a volley of shot—another—then stillness.

"The soldiers will doubtless camp in the hacienda till day," said Fray Antonio. "My child, you are shaking with chill."

"La pobrecita! The brave little one! She shall sleep in our house the night," one of the women invited kindly.

Lucia was suddenly conscious of her strange appearance there in the moonlight. Halfway to her ankle hung one leg of the breeches, and above their rowdy boyishness her mud-splattered white camisa rose incongruous. She was glad that her face was hidden by the morion. She had yanked it down with both hands to keep it from coming off, and now she could hardly see out from under it.

Making herself as small as possible, she followed Doña Catarina up one ladder, up another, across a housetop to the door. Soon she was sharing a pallet with two of Doña Catarina's daughters.

For a while she lay awake, staring into blackness. This time it was a tightly sheltered blackness, made reassuringly commonplace by the sonorous breathing of sleeping people. Lucia's body twanged all over, as if she were a harp plucked by unseen fingers; her nerves jumped and her muscles throbbed and her joints ached and her skinned places smarted. But she was safe, and without a doubt her family in the hacienda were safe also. The Indians would have retreated before the armed soldiers, to bother the Riveras no more for this time.

Lucia made a little prayer, thanking the Virgin for her blue eyes. She thanked her because the Tano posted at the edge of the thicket had been the Eagle, who had seen Domingo often enough to know that his eyes were a normal brown. She thanked her because the Eagle had never seen her, Domingo's twin, at close range, and did not guess that they were almost alike, except for size and color of eyes. She thanked her because the Eagle, nominally a Christian, had been familiar with the face of the Virgin.

He had been frightened out of his wits at seeing brown eyes changed to blue. He might even have thought Lucia the Virgin herself. Lucia crossed herself devoutly and went thankfully to sleep.

Once awake next morning, Lucia could hardly wait to go home. Fray Antonio took her, but she was disconcerted to find that they were escorted by two young men with muskets over their shoulders. Lucia walked silent and red-faced, with a borrowed shawl only half hiding her knee breeches. She kept her gaze steadily averted from the escorts, for they were none other than Salvador and Higinio.

Arriving at the estancia, they found the guards that had gone to its aid yawning and stretching and enjoyably picking their teeth. Rosa and Lupe, flushed and moist with hurry, were baking tortillas, and the remains of a leg of mutton were keeping warm at the fire. As soon as they had quite done eating, the soldiers would thoroughly patrol the region. Old Juan could safely take his flock out to the nearer grazing land.

Yet all this peace and quiet seemed only the pause between thunderbolts, the darkness between lightning flashes, so long as Domingo and Gaspar were still abroad, and Uncle Melchior.

Siesta time came, but it was siesta for none but the children. Even Tia Nina refused to lie down. She sat in an attitude of watchfulness, bolt upright on the well-curb, her chins resting on her lace neck frill, her closed lids dark with weariness.

Then horses' hoofs sounded on the road and stopped at the gate. "Hola!" shouted a boyish voice.

It was Domingo's.

Swift as shadows, Roque and Fernando were unbarring

the big gates and swinging them inward. The two youths
rode into the patio, a few turkeys and rabbits slung across
their saddles. Their matter-of-fact gaiety turned to astonishment as a flood of questions burst upon them.

"Why have you been so long away?" Tia Nina wailed,
toddling over to Domingo's horse and reaching up to
touch a bloody scratch on the boy's hand. "And have you
seen or heard aught of your uncle? How could you leave
us in such terror?"

"We are safe and sound, as you can see," her nephew
assured her, fidgeting under her hands and swinging from
his saddle. "No thanks to the rascally Tanos, though."

"Son, tell us."

"Well, it is not much to tell. We followed the deer
that Gaspar sighted. Killed two and skinned them and
had started to cut them up. Then some magpies flew
squawking off to one side. Gaspar said something must
have scared them. So we mounted. Had to leave the meat
behind, except for a leg I had just whacked off. We made
it to a high point where we could see without being seen.
And there, as we thought, Tanos."

"Hostile Tanos?" his aunt quavered.

"I do not know why else they would be in the bushes
with their bellies hugging the ground. And one of them
with a Spanish musket. They were not hunting deer, that
was plain."

Lucia, unable to contain her own news any longer, broke
in excitedly, "Luckily ours had only bows and arrows."

Domingo glanced absently at her and rattled on: "We
rode off out of range like the wind, and kept going until
at nightfall we found ourselves beyond the Black Mesa.
To say truth, we did not know exactly where we were,
for—"

"For the night was so dark, with the moon not up till late," Lucia agreed eagerly. "And lucky that was for me, for the Eagle, who had caught me, had a torch, and it shone full in my eyes, and—"

Now at last Domingo stopped talking to stare at his sister. "The Eagle, who had caught you? Did you say— the Eagle? Who caught you?"

"But she also is safe and sound, praise be," Doña Leonor's low voice interposed.

"Safe and sound, yes. But, oh, the terror! And we all defenseless and like to be butchered! And my poor heart pounding until I was near to death," Tia Nina babbled.

"Such a one, our young lady," wheezed Rosa, standing arms akimbo at the edge of the group. "Except for her, dead and buried we all might be, and without absolution." She crossed herself at the thought. "Except for her, the patio might this moment be swarming with Apaches and Tanos—"

"And she will not tell us how she got over the garden wall," Tia Nina broke in.

Roque was sweeping the walks, and, even in her excitement, Lucia noticed that his broom moved slower and slower, as if he were listening with all his might. She noticed also that Fernando was standing on one foot behind his wife, his pointed tongue running restlessly round his lips.

"The Virgin helped me," said Lucia.

"You tell us your story, my son," Doña Leonor bade him. "Then we will tell ours."

With another frown of wonder at Lucia, Domingo told. On the first night, the boys had camped in a high place, under a piñon tree. They had built a small fire, for pro-

tection from bear and puma, and for cooking. With so
many Indians of different tribes about, Gaspar felt that
smoke could not inform the hostiles that a Spaniard was
near. And they needed food, having long since finished
off the tortillas and meat they had fetched that morning
from Rosa's kitchen. They roasted the one leg of venison
that Domingo had saved when they rode away from the
Tanos. They seasoned it as best they could with saltbush and wild sage. Tough though it was, they relished it,
and filled their stomachs, and slept.

Next day they continued their hunting, though the
game was scarce even here, farther from Santa Cruz and
the pueblos. They flushed a few turkeys and shot them,
and Gaspar knocked over two jack rabbits with his Moki
throwing stick. They had worked farther south and west
as they hunted, and Gaspar feared that they were getting
into the country of the Jemez, whose friendliness he
doubted. He felt that it would be safer to return by the
Camino Real, for it was a traveled road, and fairly well
patroled. So they struck east. But they had gone so far
afield that darkness overtook them before they reached
the Royal Road. They camped another night and hurried
on in the morning. And here they were. And now, by all
twelve apostles, what was this about Lucia and the Eagle?

The chatter that followed was like that of a flock of
grackles. Everyone joined in. Rosa had established herself in a patch of shade, plump arms clasping plump body.
Roque and Fernando pressed closer and closer. Lupe
dropped her work and crowded in. Soledad came, cradling
the light weight of her ailing baby. The children dodged
under adult arms, wriggled between their fathers' legs,
came up in the midst and squatted there, listening wide-
eyed. Each grown person put in additions, corrections,

exclamations, cries of horror and admiration, while Lucia told her story.

She had barely finished when the gates resounded under a thunderous pounding and the bell clanged like mad and Uncle Melchior roared, "Open! Open!" As soon as he was safely inside, the tale of the siege had to be told all over again, this time by a trio of voices, Tia Nina's, Domingo's and Lucia's. And when that was done, Domingo related his own adventure with Gaspar.

Taking charge of Don Melchior's mount, Roque and Fernando had melted nervously away. They returned little by little, pretending complete absorption in tasks that kept them in earshot. Old Rosa and Lupe and Soledad withdrew at first to a respectful distance. Only the children stayed where they were, for they were less intimidated than their elders by Don Melchior's knotted eyebrows and by the glare of his eyes under their folds of lid. And gradually the whole crew had closed in again.

At length Uncle Melchior, sitting in his elbowchair, which Rosa had dragged out into the portal for him, drew a gusty breath and mopped his brow. "They told us at the New Town that there had been a siege, and I did not wait for details. One thing is sure: we will bring able-bodied servants up from Mexico, men who are men." He hammered the chair arm with his fist and glared at Roque and Fernando. "We will send for more muskets to come up by the next wagons, and a store of powder and shot. This kingdom is a long way from being safe; it may be years before we have the Indians subdued. They may never be wholly so in our time. But with a few more stout men and a supply of arms and ammunition, we can make this estancia as safe as a fort. And we will."

Then his eyes returned to Lucia, amazement and concern sharpening them. She was Lucia again, chestnut hair glossy, full skirt demurely covering her ankles, though her face was scratched and her lips were puffed where they had been lashed by thorny branches.

"And Lucia! I cannot credit it! Why you did not die of fright in the grasp of that Apache—under the eyes of that Tano. Muchacha, I cannot fathom it. My flesh creeps at the mere thought. We must make a novena to Our Lady. Blue—the blue of the Virgin. And more blue than ever when the light of his torch made its black pupil grow small as a pinpoint, as I have seen it do. And I had never noticed how much she grows to look like her mother, who is in turn a picture of some of the statues of Our Lady. No wonder that knavish Eagle was half-crazed with guilty terror."

"And Lucia so brave!" Tia Nina whimpered. "But so wild and hoydenish!" she added in a shocked voice, bethinking of that angle of her niece's behavior. "Whatever would the gentlefolk in Mexico City think of her, dressing herself in men's clothing? What kind of husband could she get if the story were told?"

"Husband," Uncle Melchior mused. "Yes, we had best find her a husband, before she goes turning herself into a boy outright. Also a husband would be another fighting man."

The hot blood flooded Lucia's face. A husband! She had long feared that this matter of a husband would pop up. Fifteen, going on sixteen, was old enough for marriage. Even boys of that age married. But who would be a proper husband for Lucia Rivera? In Santa Cruz there was no one who would do at all. At that thought Lucia took a relieved breath. Tio Melchior would never ally his family with any of the unmarried youths in that part of New

Mexico. Salvador, Doña Ana's loutish son; Higinio Padilla; Don Melchior would look down his nose at either of them, and they were as desirable as any within reach.

Lucia glanced at Domingo. He was frowning, as if the idea of his sister's marriage had startled him also. He did not look as if it pleased him, and neither did Gaspar. Lucia thought that her mother liked it as little as they, for she spoke more hastily than was her habit, introducing an entirely different topic.

"Old Juan," she said, "is convinced that we have Maria to thank for saving our lives."

Her words snatched Don Melchior's attention away from his niece. "Maria? What Maria is that?"

Yes, Maria diverted all minds and sent the current of talk rushing in other directions. Lucia's thoughts, and probably Domingo's, leaped at once to the paper that the Navajo woman had intrusted to Gaspar. The possibility that she was Maria made the fragmentary chart more exciting and important by far. The young people were not yet ready to admit their uncle and aunt to the secret, but, finding his mother alone after supper, Domingo drew forth the tight-folded sheet and gave it to her, his finger at his lips.

As she opened it out, Doña Leonor's face paled and quivered, and she touched the few written words with awed finger tips. "Though I cannot read them," she whispered, "I know them for the handwriting of your father, may he enjoy peace."

Reverently her son and daughter crossed themselves.

"But what then do you think it can mean?" Domingo asked, his voice shaken by the new discovery. "It says, 'Entierno de—' and that is all. What do you think my father could have buried?"

His mother shook her head, still caressing the paper. "De la plata?" Lucia eagerly suggested.

"It could be the silver. Yes, it could well be," Doña Leonor said, still dreamily. "While Rosa and I were grabbing up the food and clothing for the escape, your father was busied in the sala. I remember it now, but then, in the excitement—confusion, fear—then, it slipped from my mind as if it had never been there. Silver, possessions, they are less than nothing when one flees for life."

After they left the house of the Santa Cruz alcalde, a harried band of fugitives, they would risk no light talk. And after the arrow struck down their father, their mother would have no talk at all, but only tears.

"Gaspar and I will go to the old estancia," said Domingo, "and dig in the sala floor and see."

"I too," Doña Leonor assented. "Maria—I must know if this is truly our Maria."

Next morning the four of them set out. To Tia Nina they made the excuse that they would look for wild grapes within sight of the hacienda. Straight toward the tower they turned their steps, a quarter-mile east of the gate of Tio Melchior's hacienda, just as the entrance to the New Town was a quarter-mile to the north and west on the bending road.

When they reached the place they found it silent, basking in the October sun with the soft, warm stillness peculiar to the season.

Timidly Doña Leonor looked in at the door of the tower. It was empty.

"There is such a smell of sheep," said Lucia, sniffing.

They went on into the ruins of the old sala. At the corners the walls stood three or four feet high, but between them one could step in at will from the place where the portal had been.

"This, too, smells of sheep; and no wonder," Doña Leonor commented. "Could Old Juan have grazed ours here? Surely not, with his terror of witchcraft."

Lucia was thinking that their small flock would have taken at least a year to leave the deposit of dung through which the Riveras and Gaspar were picking their way. But she could not waste time talking about sheep when the intierno of treasure might be close at hand.

Not seeing the Navajo woman, Doña Leonor reluctantly turned her attention to the chart. When Domingo had turned it about so that its south was really south, it was to see the location Don José had probably indicated. Both boys had brought spades. Now they leaned their guns against the ruined fireplace and made ready to start digging.

Lucia stopped them. "Mother," she said coaxingly, only to pause, with her upper lip drawn down and her nose quivering. "Mother," she repeated, "we do not need a silver service. Wood and pewter have done very well, have they not?"

Her mother looked at her in mild surprise. "Are you fortifying yourself against disappointment, daughter? How wise you are growing. If anything of value was ever buried here, the Indians would probably have found it in the years between."

Lucia tossed back her chestnut hair emphatically. "No, no!" she denied. "I did not mean that at all, little mother. I meant, if we find the silver—"

Again she paused, looking past her mother at the Navajo woman, who could be seen coming from the direction of the tower. Lucia hurried on. "If we find it, Mother,

may we not sell enough of it to—to set Gaspar free?"
Though she was gazing at her mother with eager intensity,
she was still aware of the Navajo woman, who also seemed
intent upon the answer.

Doña Leonor spoke slowly. "Daughter, I think—I
think yes."

Gaspar's bronze face had reddened darkly and his lips
were pressed tight shut. With a convulsive movement
of eagerness he drove his spade deep into the debris.

By that time Doña Leonor had become aware of another
presence. Turning, she looked at the Navajo woman, and
then went to her swiftly and took both of her passive
hands, while she gazed searchingly into her face.

"Maria?" she asked; and, as if finding more and more
that was familiar in the steady eyes and gaunt, firm face,
she cried, "Maria! Our dear Maria!"

The woman had quietly returned Doña Leonor's gaze.
When the lady spoke her name, Maria bowed her forehead on the Spanish woman's shoulder and stood silent.

Chapter 15

Silver?

FOR a few minutes the two boys dug steadily. The accumulation of sheep dung was inches deep. Except for the top layer, which seemed fresh, it had grown inoffensive in the sun and dry air, and it was not so hard as to resist the iron blades. Soon, however, Gaspar paused.

"The hard adobe," he said.

Domingo labored feverishly for a little longer, and then he also stopped. "Surely the floor," he admitted with an explosive sigh. "Undisturbed, too; hard as an earthenware platter."

"But why, then, the chart?" Lucia protested.

"That is not difficult to explain," Doña Leonor said.

"Your father, God rest him, might well have made the chart before digging, and then found that there was no time to bother with silver when life itself was at stake."

"But—but to make the chart first—that seems like turning things hind side foremost," Domingo objected, still puffing from exertion. "I would rather dig up the whole floor than believe it. See, Gaspar!" With finger and thumb he traced imaginary lines on the chart. "Here would be a likely place. Or here. Let us each try one of these points."

Again they drove their spades through the surface debris, flinging it out over the broken walls. Lucia fidgeted around them, listening for some sound that might indicate that the iron had struck looser ground than the floor. Her hope flattened as Domingo's spade and then Gaspar's grated again on a firm, hard surface.

The three young heads came together, then, over the chart. While Domingo went on one knee to hold the paper against a bit of adobe hearth, Lucia scooped her skirts around her and tried to balance on her heels as Gaspar was doing.

"I say here is a likely spot," she said, pointing.

"Better here," Domingo answered.

The boys jumped up and went back to work, Domingo digging furiously in the place of his choice, Gaspar impassively in the one Lucia had suggested.

Lucia's attention was pulled from the boys to the talk of the two women and back to the boys again. Seeing Maria did her mother good, she thought tenderly. They had loved each other. And as a woman in another woman's home, Doña Leonor had not had much of a life since the Revolt, though many Spanish women had to put up with the same lot. Mother was the strong, quiet kind, and she had grown quieter and more shut in through the years. Now she looked younger, as if Maria had brought back a breath of her happy youth. She asked eager questions, and sometimes Maria replied, briefly, in Spanish that had grown rusty from disuse. Sometimes she did not answer, as when Doña Leonor inquired about her son.

"The dear little José? Is he well? How does he get about, with the lame leg? Is he big, like Domingo? Like Gaspar?"

At that, Maria lowered her eyes and said nothing. After waiting a minute, Doña Leonor went on to other questions. Had Maria married again? Yes. Had she other children? Two daughters: so big. Maria held her hand level with her shoulder; then dropped it to the height of her waist.

"Where are they?" Doña Leonor asked eagerly. "Maria, how I long to see them!"

"Maybe tomorrow. Maybe tomorrow I bring them here," replied Maria evasively.

"And your husband?"

A new sound from the excavating operations interrupted her, and sent Lucia scurrying to Gaspar's side. His spade had struck a different substance. It scraped, as on wood, and grated, as on metal. The three young people pushed against each other, trying to see the prize.

"Do keep from underfoot, Lucia," Domingo begged. "We men will loosen it and lift it out."

More digging: spades moving cautiously, earth flying wildly over the remnants of wall.

"Now!" cried Domingo, dropping his tool with a clatter and plumping down on the ground at his side of the hole.

Reaching down and fumbling for the iron rings at the ends of the buried object, the boys rose, grunting, to their knees and heaved. The box came up so lightly that they had to scramble to keep their balance. Watching, wide-eyed and breathless, Lucia felt a cold misgiving. Surely the Rivera silver would be heavier than this.

The boys deposited the box on the littered floor and straightened to look at it. It was a stout wooden chest of the style so much used by the Hispanos, painted all over in designs of red, blue and ochre. Domingo tugged at the lid. It resisted his hand.

"I remember the chest. And the key," Doña Leonor spoke on a drawn breath. "The key was always among your father's belongings. You will have to force the lock."

The boys tipped the chest backward, Domingo shaking his head as if he also were uneasy at its light weight, and at the muffled sound its shifting contents gave forth. Each boy thrust his spade into the crack under the lid, and put his weight on the handle. With a shriek of reluctant iron, the lid sprang open.

Out of the tilted box rolled a clumsy bundle of white and black wool carpeting.

"Silver!" Lucia shrieked triumphantly.

Cautiously the boys unrolled the carpeting and pulled it straight, until its contents lay revealed on the lid of the chest. Lucia drew a deep breath and bent closer. This was not the family plate.

Doña Leonor gasped. "Holy things from the old church!" she whispered. "I remember them well. How Fray Antonio will rejoice! These are far richer and finer than anything he has for the new church. In the early days Spain and Mexico possessed more wealth than now, and then nothing was too precious for the worship of God and His blessed Mother."

The five crowded round to look. Inside the swaddling folds was another wrapping, this one of shimmering Chinese brocade, iridescent as a handful of gems. Nested in the brocade lay a golden monstrance, delicately worked, and with semiprecious stones around the glassed-in relic, a lock of hair evidently from the head of a saint long dead. Beside the monstrance was a chalice of beaten silver, tarnished to deep gray and darkly rainbowed by the years. There were, besides, a silver paten inlaid with jewel-bright enamel, and, carefully folded, a chasuble of heavy silk, intricately embroidered in pictured panels of gold and silver colored threads.

"Fray Antonio will look the Prince of God indeed, cloaked in this magnificence to celebrate the Mass. And was it not like your father," murmured Doña Leonor, lifting her rebozo to wipe away the tears, "yes, exactly like him, to protect the things of Holy Church before his own possessions. Not that he would have failed to protect our treasure also, had there been time enough. But Holy Church came first."

"Surely he buried the silver somewhere else!" Domingo cried out in a voice ragged with disappointment. "Let us dig farther. Come, Gaspar, we will dig up the whole floor, if need be."

Slowly Gaspar took up his spade. His face was a mask, and out of its pallor burned the branded R. He had hoped, Lucia thought, for freedom; longed for it with an inner sickness.

Maria spoke so decisively that they all turned toward her. "No. Don José not bury those family dishes." Her words marched with the sad finality of a funeral procession. "The dishes stand there," she went on, shooting out her chin toward the ruined hearth. "The silver plates. The pitcher and bowl. The forks and spoons. Also the chocolate cups, not silver but like eggshells, and with colored flowers. I remember well. There they stand, as if he would hide them. Then you call, Doña Leonor. You call him to make haste and save himself."

They waited, Lucia's heart thundering with hope. Perhaps Maria would say that she herself had hidden the silver.

No, Maria's words were still the funeral march. "Next day I come back. I come still and careful. I am afraid, but I think maybe I save those things for Don José. But no. The Pueblos had come first. Everything gone. All Don José's fine things."

To Maria they were Don José's things. How often Mother had said, half-laughing, "She worshiped your father as if he had been a saint. And perhaps he was."

"Yes, all gone. Only a few papers. Like that one." Maria pointed at the chart.

"You did not keep the papers?" Doña Leonor asked.

Maria made a sound that might mean no.

Exploding into something between sob and groan, Domingo hurled his spade on the ground. "But these which are silver," he muttered thickly. "They could be melted down. The silver might be enough to—to ransom Gaspar."

Lucia's tears went dry and she looked hopefully at her mother. Doña Leonor's face was white and sorrowful.

"My son! When your father risked his life to save these treasures for the Church, how can you think for one moment of diverting them to other uses? They are a trust. Before God they are a trust. Think fairly in your heart. Would it not be a theft from God himself? Would it not be black sin?"

Penitence for her unspoken thoughts had already turned Lucia's joints to jelly, but Domingo's face did not soften.

"Is it a blacker sin than keeping a man like Gaspar in slavery?" he asked sullenly. "Of late the scar on his brow burns my own flesh."

Doña Leonor's eyes were steady upon him. "Your father might have felt the same pain. But to sell the chalice, the paten, would that not be committing one sin to undo another? No, we must take these things to Fray Antonio, to the church, where they belong. And you must confess to the padre your sinful thought."

"All these things? All?" Domingo muttered, pushing at the striped carpeting with his toe.

"Why not? Nothing of it is ours, except the carpet, which Rosa doubtless wove when our servant, and the silk. The silk might one day be a wedding gown for Lucia."

For a fleeting moment Lucia pictured the brocade, fashioned into an overdress and looped back to show, perhaps, a puffed and flounced underdress of rosy silk, with little velvet bows marching up the front from hem to bodice.

"Will you go with me, then?" Domingo's face was dark and resisting, but his eyes held a small-boy look as he glanced under drooping lids at his mother.

In the end, Doña Leonor and Lucia accompanied Domingo to Santa Cruz, and Gaspar went along to help with the chest. The two boys carried it between them to the estancia, and then loaded it into the carreta, quietly, so as to save explanations to the household. Doña Leonor and Lucia rode with the new-found treasure, and Gaspar drove the oxen, while Domingo walked Oro slowly behind.

They found Fray Antonio with his catechism class, but at the urgency in their faces he went with them at once to the vestry.

There the boys set down the chest, and Domingo silently opened it.

Fray Antonio sucked in his breath and dropped on his knees beside the treasure. Reverently he opened out the chasuble, spreading it over the lid of the chest. Reverently he set the monstrance, the chalice, the paten, on a table and studied them with rapt eyes.

"So do the holy objects return to their own place," he murmured. "I have heard of these. Some have said that the monstrance was the work of Benvenuto Cellini, and priceless. Whence came they now, Señora?"

"From where my husband, may he enjoy peace, concealed them the day before he received his mortal wound," Doña Leonor answered. "Before his household treasure did he prize the treasure of Holy Church, and guard it."

"But why sorrow on faces where there should be naught but joy?" the padre inquired, looking keenly from one to the other.

Lucia glanced apprehensively at her brother. His lips seemed stiff with unwillingness, but after a moment he spoke.

"Padre, my mother feels that I have committed a sin."

"So? And how is that?"

"I thought the good Lord would let me have the chalice and the paten." Domingo stopped, head down, as if unable to say more.

Lucia's tremulous voice came to his rescue. "Fray Antonio, we thought if we could melt down the silver and have the price of it—"

The padre stopped her, his eyes flashing, his hand lifted. "Sin indeed!" he cried. "The besetting sin of our people, the sin of greed, the lust for gold. And you two, the ones of my children whom I should least have suspected of the taint! You, who have, besides, more of this world's goods than any other settlers hereabouts! I cannot credit it."

Domingo seemed petrified, and Lucia's sense of guilt thickened her tongue and clogged her thoughts. Fear stifled her, also, for Fray Antonio's anger was terrible. It was not like their Uncle Melchior's rage, a sullen, smoldering fire that could snap and flame but which was human and understandable. And it gave the brother and sister small chance to put in a word in their own defense, but swept on overpoweringly.

"Already many of our settlers have reached the end of their supplies. The promised goods do not come from Mexico. This may be another calamitous winter. There have been such winters before, when the people had to cut old sheepskins into strips and boil them for food; when they must needs sell their clothing to the Indians for maize, and go freezing in the storm.

"You have warm clothes and a comfortable home, and you cannot starve, since if worse comes to worst you can butcher your sheep. And yet it is you—you—who contemplate this sin! You, Domingo, whom I have come to regard as my spiritual son, you prove as badly corrupted by this accursed hunger for riches as the most ignorant soldier. How can you excuse such rapacity?"

While the three Riveras stood mute, Gaspar spoke. "Father—"

The padre's eyes turned to him questioningly. "Yes, my son?"

"Padre, it was not for themselves. It was for me."

"For you?" Fray Antonio's mounting wrath dropped suddenly to bewilderment.

Seeing that Gaspar had said all he would, Doña Leonor completed his explanation. "My children have wished to buy Gaspar. For some time now they have wished to buy the youth from their uncle, so that they might set him free. Don Melchior is a good man," she added, "and honest in all his dealings. It is not strange that he should see the matter only as a business transaction. Our Spanish gentlemen, as you well know, have been brought up to despise gentleness and softness."

The padre wiped his brow, pushing back the moist strands of red-gold hair that clung to its white expanse. "God forgive me," he murmured. "I am too quick to take fire."

At this Lucia found courage to drop on her knees and take his hand in supplication. "You yourself said that men should not be bought and sold like sheep," she said in a small choked voice. "And especially not Gaspar. Gaspar, I think, is brighter even than Domingo; and better. And we have no money, Domingo and I. Do you not think the good God will forgive us if our thought was sinful?"

Fray Antonio's other hand rested on her head. Solemnly he bowed his own, assenting. "And as for Gaspar, my daughter," he said, "we will think what can be done. We will ask the good God and Our Lady to show us the way."

Chapter 16

In the Haunted Tower

NEXT morning Doña Leonor, Domingo, Lucia and Gaspar went again to the old hacienda. Once more they assuaged Tia Nina's curiosity and pacified her by promising to search for late wild grapes, which they had entirely forgotten the day before.

Doña Leonor was all eagerness to see Maria's little girls. Domingo and Lucia darted surprised glances at their mother and at each other as they hurried along the road through the fallen leaves—yellow leaves from the cottonwoods, bronze and red from the cherry trees, and flaming variegated ones from the peach trees. They were accustomed to seeing their mother gentle and sweet and strong, but never gay. Now she hummed a snatch of an old ballad, and her eyes shone.

"Maria may have forgotten," Lucia suggested, afraid to see Doña Leonor disappointed.

Doña Leonor's tone was confident. "Maria will not forget."

But when they turned in from the road there was no sign of the Navajo woman. The tower glowed in the soft October sunshine, and crested jays swooped on broad blue wings, and chickadees flitted and called, and crickets sang sleepily. But of human life there was no sign.

Doña Leonor leaned against one of the standing corners of wall and said cheerfully, "She will come in good time."

"Si, Señora, I am here."

The quiet words startled the three Riveras. Maria had approached from the direction of the tower, and with her were the daughter who came to her shoulder, the daughter who came to her waist. Their eyes were wide with a shyness akin to terror, and they flattened themselves against their mother as if to sink out of sight in the scant folds of her dress.

"Oh, las pobrecitas, they are afraid of us!" Lucia cooed, running over and dropping on her knees before them, while they crowded tighter than ever to their mother.

Doña Leonor spoke almost as cooingly. "Las hermosisimas! Las queridas! We must take care not to frighten them, the darlings. Maria, what are they called?"

"The tall one is Leonor," Maria answered. "In the Dinneh tongue she is Tlitchiebah. The small one is Lucia— and Nazbah."

Lucia shrieked her delight, and Lucia-Nazbah shrank completely out of sight at the sound. "Oh," Lucia mourned, "be not afraid, little one." She sat back on her heels, hands spread on skirts, and blinked beguilingly whenever one of her Navajo namesake's great, lustrous brown eyes ventured out of hiding.

"They do not yet know the Spanish language," Maria explained.

Lucia had noticed that Maria spoke her Spanish words one by one, just as Gaspar did, though her Dinneh speech came in a swift current. Always the Indian's Spanish moved in a procession rather than flowing in a stream.

"We must make our namesakes little Mexican camisas and petticoats," Doña Leonor said tenderly. "Though to be sure they are nicely clothed, Maria."

"Woolen tunics," Lucia commented. "Woolen."

The little girls were winsome in straight black wool frocks like their mother's, drawn together and tied on the right shoulder and leaving the other shoulder bare. The garments were simply blankets, folded round their bodies and girt with stoutly woven cotton belts in red and white. The clothing was so clean that Lucia thought it must be new, since the firm wool was hard to wash. Their high red-brown leather moccasins also were new, and their well-brushed hair was drawn back and wrapped with clean cotton cord like their mother's.

"They are dolls," Lucia crooned, "little Apache du Navahu dolls."

She would have liked to ask Maria where she had got the wool for their dresses and her own, but that did not seem a delicate question, in view of the great flock that had been given over to Maria at the time of the Revolt. To be sure, fifteen years had elapsed, and that flock could be gone twice over, to the wolves and the coyotes, the bobcats and the cougars, the drought, the blizzard, the Apaches, Comanches and Utes.

"Gaspar," Doña Leonor said, "do you suppose if you were to ask her in her own language, and make it clear to her that she is very dear to us, do you think perhaps she would tell us about José?"

Gaspar was silent for a moment, as if he were turning the question over until he was sure of its shape and substance. Then he spoke swiftly to Maria, while she stood poised and easy, her eyes moving from Gaspar to the distance and back. As if to show that she was following, she interposed an occasional "Ah—ah—ah." When Gaspar ceased speaking, she was still, too, with a contemplative stillness, one of her slim brown hands stroking back her smaller daughter's hair.

"We do not speak much of the dead," Gaspar explained abruptly. "It is the old Dinneh way. Not to speak of death. Or sickness. Or misfortune. We have been taught so; that our Holy Ones like yes better than no."

"Your Holy Ones!" Doña Leonor remonstrated. "But you and Maria are baptized Christians, Gaspar."

"Yes," Gaspar agreed, crossing himself. "But we are also Dinneh, Señora."

Maria brought her long-awaited reply into the conversation. "José," she said, "José grew tall. Like Don Domingo. Almost a man, he was. He looked like Gaspar, a little. But always lame."

Was.

"And your husband?" Doña Leonor asked compassionately.

"He was a good man," Maria said simply. "And he help good with the sheep."

It was her first mention of the sheep.

"His brothers also help me. Ever the Apaches watch. They steal when they could. So we needed men. For two

summers we were up yonder. At the Place of the Rocks."
Maria tossed her head backward and sidewise, indicating
probably the mighty slash of Canyon de Tse. There had
been rumors that it was a Navajo home and fortress, the
tribe being weak in numbers.

"Why did you go so far?" asked Doña Leonor.

"Because most of the people were afraid. Afraid of
the Spanish. Some of the Dinneh had taken sides with
the Pueblos. When they drove the Spanish from the
Kingdom. Then we hear that the Spanish come back.
With soldiers and guns and the big General. We were
afraid what might happen to us. But my Hasteen and
my son, they not killed by the Spanish. It was Comanches,
coming after the sheep. Hasteen and José, they fought
for the sheep. They also had grown to love them. They
fought, but they were two against many."

"And you returned here alone, my poor Maria," Doña
Leonor said pitifully. "Were you not afraid?"

Again Maria stood long silent, as if arranging her
thoughts and preparing her reply. Domingo, sprawling
on a length of crumbled wall, was listening with complete
absorption. Gaspar sat on his heels, eyeing the ground.
In the interval Lucia absently wooed the children, chirping
to them softly. Both had come out into the open now,
and Leonor-Tlitchiebah reached out and touched the embroidery at Lucia's neck, pulling back her small finger
quickly, as if the frill had pricked her, and giggling a tiny,
explosive giggle.

At last Maria replied.

"My man's young brothers return with me. We hear
that the Spanish are coming to live again at Santa Cruz.
I think, maybe Don José come, and Doña Leonor, and
those babies." She let her glance flick Domingo and Lucia

with a suggestion of dry humor. "And the padre, Fray Antonio, he is good."

"But why did you not come to us, Maria?" Doña Leonor asked.

"No Don José," Maria explained. "And instead Don Melchior and his fat, soft woman. And then the Hispanos saying I am a witch."

"Maria," Lucia cried, so abruptly that both little girls melted into their mother's tunic again, "who made the strange fire in the tower? The dreadful light?"

Maria smiled. "It is good secret, no? And I think it not only save me. It scare away that soldier who wanted Don José's rancho for his own. He tell me about the soldier," she added, with a chin thrust toward Gaspar.

"Maria," Doña Leonor said wistfully, "if only I and my children could rebuild the old house and live here again in our own place! Then, too, our little flock would prosper. And we should prosper. I am sure of it."

The hunger and the homesickness in her face seemed to move Maria. With the children clinging to her and hampering her, so that she put them aside with hands gently firm, Maria went to the broken wall beside the fragment of fireplace. There her fingers pried at the adobe bricks. Doña Leonor and the boys watched questioningly, and Lucia twisted round on her knees, her mouth open.

With both hands, Maria lifted out one of the large bricks, and from behind it some scraps of paper. These she laid silently in Doña Leonor's hand, which came out, palm up, to receive them. Breathing hard, Domingo and Lucia jostled each other in their haste to see the fragments as their mother leafed through them.

"They were partly burned," Domingo stammered. "Is there anything of importance?"

Doña Leonor scrutinized a ragged piece with a fragment of red sealing wax still adhering to it. Two lines of flourishing old script remained, grown pale brown with age.

"—ey de la Espana, anno Domine 1608—" Domingo read aloud—"Mother! This looks like—"

Doña Leonor swallowed as if her throat were too dry for speech. All the firm, clear contours of her face crumpled and went soft. "True. It is all that remains of the old grant. I remember it well. 'Philip the Second,' it was signed. Your father told me. Philip the Second, 'el rey,' the king of Spain. And the royal rubric I could never forget." With a finger she traced a flourish, like a long-tailed *C*, the rubric, which was always an individual part of every signature, its grand ending. "It was the grant to your father's grandfather, God rest them both: Don Fidel Anastasio Asuncion Maria y José de Rivera y Salazar."

"And no good now, no good at all," Lucia mourned.

Kneeling there in the sweet sunshine, with late purple asters pushing into the ruined casa, and rabbit brush fluffy with white seed, Lucia longed more powerfully than ever before for this home of their own. She knew that her mother was pierced by the same homesickness.

"We shall get a new grant." Doña Leonor spoke with certainty and fire. "Since Maria has scared away our greedy soldier, there is little to stand in our way. We shall make petition again to His Excellency the Governor." She smiled at Maria. "Then would you come, Maria? You and your daughters? And your husband's brothers? Would you help Old Juan with our poor little flock? With you to aid me I should have courage indeed."

Lucia drew a deep breath. Domingo threw an arm across their mother's shoulder. They waited.

Maria stood unspeaking, eyes cast down.

Chapter 17

The Silver Treasure

THE PAUSE grew longer, longer and tighter.
To break its tautness, Lucia said, "Poor Tío Melchior! Will he think we are not fond of him, when we leave his roof, Mother?" She felt a growing tenderness for her uncle and aunt, now that escape was in sight.

Doña Leonor said, "We shall have good times together, once we are apart. You will see. They have been good to us. And it will be a relief to them, too—"

The minutes went on lengthening, and still Maria neither accepted nor rejected Doña Leonor's invitation.

When at last she spoke, it was only to ask, "Maybe you would like to see the tower?"

With a sibilant "S-s-s-o-o-o!" to her children, which sent them skimming along, straight-backed and swift before her, she led the way, the Riveras and Gaspar following.

The ground floor of the tower was as deep in sheep dung as the ruined rooms of the old house. Against the inner wall leaned one of the familiar ladders of the Pueblos, with tapering tree trunks for poles, and shorter lengths thrust through holes in the sidepieces. The little girls scurried up it, ahead of their mother, and the rest strung out behind, not to crowd the ladder, which sprung under their weight.

Lucia, preceding Domingo, stopped and gasped when her head rose above the hatchway.

"Vete! Do hasten!" Domingo cried, and reached up to give her ankles an impatient pinch.

Hurriedly she drew herself up and the boys followed. They stood in a circular room of Indian masonry with a clay floor and with a slit of a window facing each way, north, west, south and east. Benches with slab tops ran around the adobe-plastered wall, and another ladder led upward, evidently to the roof.

To all this Lucia gave a casual glance. What interested and astonished her was the loom, hanging against the wall where the light was best. It was, of course, a simple loom. A roof log formed the top of its frame, and the other pieces were shaped from small tree trunks. At the bottom showed a few inches of weaving, the beginning of a new blanket.

"Why, you are weaving beautifully, Maria!" Doña Leonor's voice was warmly friendly, even though it held a question. "This is your work?"

"Yes, Señora. My daughter Leonor, she also learns," she added. "The Moki come to the Place of the Rock, and we learn their way also. And my Lucia is carding for her mother."

A small loom hung between two windows, with a little blanket half woven.

"How very-very nice!" Doña Leonor approved.

Under the visitors' attention, Leonor-Tlitchiebah flattened herself against the wall, her eyes closing desperately, but her mouth widening in an uncontrollable smile.

"And little Lucia is carding!" Lucia Rivera cried.

Thereupon the Navajo Lucia went groping frantically backward for the protection of her mother's skirts, and sat down suddenly on the floor.

From the ceiling poles hung twists of wool, colored and uncolored. Lucia eyed them with interest, for everything concerned with weaving had grown important to her. Here were grayish-white wool of the most ordinary sort, the rusty black of the black sheep, and the peculiar reddish brown of the prized "red sheep." Here was a rosier red, such as she herself had made from pigweed, and there a dim blue, which might have been extracted from larkspur, and a green from oak, and a yellow from rabbit brush.

Questions were crowding Lucia's mind, crowding till she thought they would burst from her. How had Maria come by such quantities of wool? It would take many churros, with their scanty fleece, to supply so much.

And how was it that this tower seemed to be a fixed habitation? Sheepskins were spread in front of the looms and where little Lucia's wool cards lay. There was a fire pit sunk in the floor, with a few glowing coals and some blackened cooking pottery in it. And now Maria was sliding back one of the slabs that covered the bench around the wall, disclosing storage chests. She was lifting out a folded blanket. She smoothed it with one hand as it lay across her arm, regarding it with satisfaction.

"Oh, Maria, it is beautiful!" Lucia cried, running to examine its gray ground and blue stripes with zigzags of yellow running through them and diamonds in black between.

"As finely woven as yours, Gaspar, or perhaps finer!" Doña Leonor praised it.

Maria held it out to her. "I have made it for you, Señora."

"Muchas-muchas gracias!" Doña Leonor said gratefully. If her eyes, lifted from the double armful of blanket, held the same perplexity that Lucia was feeling, her words did not express it. "Hold this a moment, daughter," she said. And when Lucia had taken the heavy blanket, Doña Leonor fumbled at the neck of her dress, and drew out her necklace, of tenderly colored coral.

"You also must have a gift, Maria mia," she said. "In the old days you admired these corals of mine. Wear them for me. Coral brings health and happiness."

Maria did not say thank you in words, but she dropped the string of beads over her sleek black head and looked down at them as they lay against her coppery skin and the black of her tunic. Finally she said, doubtfully considering Doña Leonor's pointed shoes, "Señora, I have more to show you. Can you walk a little way?"

"De cierto," Doña Leonor answered in a surprised voice.

Without more words, Maria swiftly descended the ladder, closely followed by her Lucia, who made small mutterings and twitterings of fear lest she be left behind. Leonor was by this time sufficiently mistress of herself to wait and follow close upon the Spanish Lucia's hands, though she cast frightened glances upward at the two youths who were last on the ladder.

Once down, Maria gestured with chin and lips to the northeast, and led the company in that direction.

"Caramba!" Lucia murmured to her brother, as she stepped full on a mass of cactus, and felt a thorn push in between the sole of her shoe and its upper. "Does she take us to see another house, think you? Or what? Do you know, Gaspar?"

With a blank face Gaspar said, "Whullah?" in Navajo, interpreting it with the Spanish "Quien sabe?" and illustrating with the shrugged shoulders that mean "Who knows?" in any language. Gaspar, Lucia decided impatiently, might know exactly where Maria was leading them, or he might not know at all. Though in the past months he had grown more at ease with the three of them, he could still shut his face against them when he wished.

By a traveled trail they were crossing a rise of ground. Sheep had passed there, Lucia thought. She could see her mother, ahead of her, looking here and there as if seeking known and loved places.

When they came to a little crest, Doña Leonor threw up a joyous hand.

"My son! My daughter!" she called back over her shoulder. "Well do I remember this! Over yonder. Let me see. When we have followed this trail a bit farther, I will show you where Old Juan liked best to keep his flock in the winter."

She was hurrying onward as she spoke, and her children caught up with her and pressed eagerly forward, while Maria strode lithely in the lead, her little girls at her side.

"There is a natural corral, a great saucer-shaped hollow,"

Doña Leonor continued. "It could be closed with a few
logs. Also, it had a south-facing slope, and sheep thrive
on a south slope. And two or three armed men could
keep off even a band of wild Indians. Now," her breath
caught "from this curve we should see the place—"

Her words faded, and she and Domingo and Lucia
all stood staring. There was the natural corral, as Doña
Leonor had described it. And in it, milling about as if
eager for release, were sheep: a great mass of grayish,
yellowish bodies, with a few that were densely black, a
few that were rust-red. Off to one side three Navajo
men lounged against a boulder and eyed the visitors.

"Maria!" Doña Leonor ejaculated. "This is the largest
flock I have seen in many a day. Two thousand, I should
guess. Whose can they be?"

Lucia's breath was gathered up and held tight as she
awaited Maria's answer. Domingo was staring incredulous.
Across the intervening space the familiar talk of the flock
reached them, the thin pipe of last spring's lambs, the
cocky bleat of a goat, the gargling and snorting of ewes.

"Whose sheep, Señora? Of a truth, they are yours."

Maria had a look of weariness as she answered, but no
longer any uncertainty. Lucia, in her pell-mell scurry
of thoughts, was sure that they would never know the
whole story. Had Maria intended to keep the flock? Had
she felt that fighting for it and suffering for it and losing
husband and son for it had made it her own?

Had she thought that Doña Leonor and Domingo and
Lucia might have grown as indifferent and cold as Don
Melchior, since their generous, kindly father was no longer
with them? Had she been persuaded otherwise by their
regard for Gaspar—Gaspar, whom she had come to love
for his likeness to her lost José?

Meanwhile, Doña Leonor stood there in the bright October sun, the tears running down her face. Gulping back a sob, she steadied her lips between her teeth. "Half of them may be ours, Maria," she said. "But half are surely yours."

Maria beckoned the Navajo men, and they strode toward the group. They were good-looking Indians, Lucia thought, almost as handsome as Gaspar. Though no one else had quite Gaspar's straight, bright gaze through furry-thick lashes; no one else his infrequent flashing smile.

"Mother," cried Lucia, bethinking herself, "now we can sell sheep enough to set him free."

"True," her mother answered. "We will do that first of all. Before even we rebuild. Before we petition for our new grant."

Glancing shyly at Gaspar, Lucia saw him straighten as if a burden had rolled from his young shoulders. He was wearing around his forehead a red banda that hid the scar, but no scar could have humbled the new pride that was in him.

The three other Navajos stood at ease before them. All were studying one another, the Spanish with open eagerness and interest, the strange Navajos with veiled hostility. As Maria spoke rapidly, evidently telling them that half the flock was still to be hers, the younger men's faces cleared, but the oldest of the three seemed less easily satisfied. He shot questions at Maria: questions that plunged abruptly downward; questions punctuated by flexible lip motions toward Doña Leonor and Domingo; masterful questions.

Maria was not awed by them. She answered with calm assurance. He shifted his weight and growled a relaxed assent.

"He is my husband," Maria told Doña Leonor.

"Your husband? But I thought your husband—"

"He is my third husband. I only lately marry him. Now we shall go to Fray Antonio. He will marry us Belliganeh way."

The Spanish group stared awkwardly at the new husband. Maria's contemplation was calmly pleased.

"He is strong!" she said, underscoring the word with an admiring rise and stress of her voice. "He is afraid of no man and of no thing. And he has a musket that he shoots so well that all men fear him. That is why I choose him," she finished complacently.

"Maria," Doña Leonor said, "would they be willing to run our sheep with yours, and be our people?"

Once more the Riveras held their collective breath. Doña Leonor's face shone with such hope that Lucia ached for her mother. But what wonder that Doña Leonor waited with her heart in her eyes? Three strong and fearless men added to their number; and Maria; and a thousand sheep in addition to the paltry handful that Old Juan was herding—

They breathed again, for Maria answered promptly. She did not even pause to consult the new husband. She said, "Si. That is what I wish, Señora."

Now all stood looking at the flock. The Navajos had not yet learned much about bettering the breed, though Maria had made good use of her months of training under Old Juan, before the Revolt. The sheep were the smallest, lightest, commonest of common churros, their fleeces loose and thin, their bellies almost bare. They would not shear more than a pound to a sheep, and each one that was killed would give a meager weight of meat. They stood facing toward the people on the trail, horned heads curiously pricked up, eyes sad and stupid. But—a thousand! A thousand Rivera sheep!

And, grazing near Tio Melchior's casa, Old Juan's handful, with their stockier bodies, their fuller and closer fleece; Old Juan's handful, with which he would gradually breed up the whole flock. There was Silver, the finest of them all. Silver would father lambs like himself, and they in turn would bring new lambs, until the Rivera flocks should stretch on and on in a foaming silver sea. Five thousand sheep—ten thousand. Sheep for this new world.

"The hidden silver—it is far better than the Rivera plate," Lucia cried thankfully. "It is the Treasure of the Silver Fleece!"